WAR

Satan's Pride

by

A.G.Kirkham

War

Copyright © 2019 AK Publishing

All rights reserved. No part of this book may be reproduced by any mechanical, photographic, or electronic process or in the form of phonographic recording; nor may it be stored in a retrieval system, transmitted, or otherwise copied for public or private use without the prior written permission of the author.

AK Publishing
Aurora, Ontario, Canada
www.romancebyagkirkham.com

Kirkham, A.G., 1965 –
WAR: Satan's Pride Series
A.G. Kirkham

Kate Struder, Editor
Dawn James (Publish and Promote),
Perseus Design, Interior Layout & Design,
Franny Armstrong, Cover Design

Printed and bound in the USA
ISBN 978-1-999-1311-1-1 (Paperback)
ISBN 978-1-999-1311-0-4 (eBook)

Note to the reader: This book is a work of fiction. The characters, organizations, events and places portrayed in this book are products of the author's imagination and are either fictitious or are used fictitiously. Any similarity to a real person, living or dead is purely coincidental and not intended by the author. The information is provided for entertainment and inspirational purposes only. In the event, you use any of the information in this book for yourself, which is your constitutional right, the author and publisher assumes no responsibility for your actions.

Contents

Acknowledgments

Thank you, Rick, for believing in me. Thank you to my children (Giulia and Antonio), my best gal pals (Karen, Laurie, Sandra and Devanne), and my sister-in-law (Cindy) who is really a sister. You have all been my inspiration and whose consistent support and optimism helped make this dream come true.

Thank you, Franny Armstrong, for the beautiful book jacket. Your hard work and extreme patience is greatly appreciated.

To Kate Studer from Proper Paper Editorial, my editor extraordinaire; whose patience, hard work, persistence, opinions, honesty, and intelligence many times inspired me.

To Dawn James, my go-to everything! Your push was what I needed to move forward with my plans and your support gave me the courage to push through.

CHAPTER 1

Can't Stop the Feeling

War

"War?" A rugged voice crackles on the other end of the phone line.

I recognize fellow Satan's Pride club member, Guard's voice immediately. "Yeah?"

"Ava wants The Smoking Guns for the party—including Maddie."

Sighing deeply, I'm dreading the way this conversation is going to go. "I tried, man. You know I would do anything for Ava, but their guitarist, Maddie's brother, Paul, said she isn't into it."

Guard and his old lady Ava's anniversary party is set to be the biggest and baddest the Satan's Pride MC had ever thrown. But I'm having trouble securing Ava's favorite band, The Smoking Guns. The celebration is to be a coming together of all the neighbouring MCs.

I

It all started when Ava risked her life to protect her man and the members of Satan's Pride against a rival club. This made Ava the "Queen" of old ladies. When a woman dedicates herself to the Pride and her love, she becomes a sister to all.

"Listen, War," Guard's tone is stern, "My wife is pregnant and moody. This is our first anniversary and her only request is for Maddie and The Smoking Guns. You need to make it happen! Offer more money. Find a way—keep it friendly though," he adds, stressing the *friendly* part.

"I was friendly. Her brother says she's really shy and only does a few concerts a year these days. Apparently, some asshole took her and held her hostage. Did enough damage that she doesn't want the gig. I offered more money; she's doesn't want that either. I offered connections and she doesn't want those. Paul says she just wants to make music. Fuck if I know what that means." I'm fed up with the whole thing. I'm used to getting what I want when I want it without negotiating. The whole concept of "asking nicely" has been torture to my badass biker soul.

"Take a meeting with Paul. I'll come too. Make it tomorrow afternoon."

I have a feeling Guard isn't going to take no for an answer.

We arrive at the only decent recording studio in the area the following day. The simple décor with clean simple furniture consists of a coffee brown reception desk, several chairs, and sofa in cream and tan off to the right. To accent the simplicity are green ferns and plants throughout the small area. In behind the reception is a hallway that leads to the actual studios.

"Hey guys," Paul greets us, extending his hand to shake each of ours as he heads toward us. I know we look intimidating; two brawny bikers wearing official Satan's Pride jeans, t-shirts, and motorcycle boots, along with our MC vests. We figured a little visual intimidation couldn't hurt.

"Hey," Guard growls, nodding toward Paul as he approaches. "Listen, we wanna talk to you about that gig the MC wants to book." He pauses before continuing, his tone suddenly more determined. "We need the whole band to be there. Anything else is not acceptable. My wife wants, and deserves, the best and I intend to give her just that."

Paul takes a step back, eying us with the look of a man who doesn't want to piss off the biggest MC in the area. Satan's Pride has a reputation and although the club has made an effort to help the town, nobody wants to get on our bad side.

Paul raises his hands in a calming manner. "I've tried to reason with Maddie," he says, keeping his voice low. "I don't know what else I can do. You think we don't want your money or this gig? We do. Maddie doesn't. I'm at my wit's end." He pauses to run a hand through his hair. "My sister only wants to make music here in the studio. Concerts are something she limits because she hates doing them."

"Let me talk to her," Guard requests, though it sounds more like a demand. He stands with his legs slightly parted, his arms crossed over his massive chest.

Paul runs a hand down his face, clearly frustrated. "You're not listening to me. This gig would scare the hell out of her. Maddie is skittish. Some shit went down at a concert a couple of years back and ever since, Maddie doesn't feel safe up on stage. When we told her this gig would be for a bunch of drunk, rowdy bikers, she vetoed the whole thing. Normally we vote, but Maddie dug her heels in and though she thinks we're the show and she's an add-on, she's the main vocal sound. We have tried everything and even promised her she would never be alone. We told her that she could leave immediately afterward. I don't know what else to do." Paul throws his hands in the air in frustration. "The rest of us can be there if you want us."

"Where is she?" I ask, finally breaking my silence. I've let Guard do the talking because I've had my fill of "nice" conversations since the negotiations with Paul began. I am tired of playing games.

"In there, recording." Paul points to the studio. "She's very vulnerable right now. She has been ever since the incident. Definitely not the rocker chick everyone sees on stage or in the videos. She only does that when it's necessary to promote our image." As Paul leads us into the recording booth he says, "I am really proud of how she has fought back the fear and steps out on the stage when she does. She is a survivor. If you stand in this spot, she won't see you." He points to a place in the booth and Guard and I move to it.

Paul hits the microphone that broadcasts into the recording room. "Maddie, can you do the last verse for me again? I wanna check the sound."

Maddie turns around and I suddenly find myself speechless. My mouth is dry. She looks much younger than her twenty-nine years. A natural beauty for sure, with long auburn hair and natural curls that reach down her curvy figure to touch her lower back. Her eyes are huge and a brilliant shade of blue. Her perfect full lips look like they were made for kissing. As I watch her, she bites down on the lower one, as though she's tempting me. I admire her simple boy-cut jeans and loose-fitting, black, capped-sleeve top as she approaches the microphone looking petite compared to the pair of blonde model-type backup singers.

"Ready?" she asks quietly.

"On three." Paul holds up his hand and counts them down. 1-2-3.

The smooth, sexy, soulful voice that emerges from such a tiny woman hits me like a sledge hammer; I am completely drawn into her. I can't tear my eyes away.

Midnight warrior, you're what I need.

Fire feeds your existence,

Lead me on, oh baby, lead me home to you.

Paul mutes the volume and faces where the two of us wait near the door before returning his attention to the mic.

"Maddie, it sounds good. Take a break. I'll be just a minute."

Paul passes by Guard and I and we follow him back out into the main entrance.

"That's Maddie," he says with his hands outstretched. "Not what you expected right?"

"Fuck. No wonder Ava wants her," I reply. My eyes feel hazy as though I've been dreaming. give my head a shake, trying to refocus and knock the haze out.

"Bring her out here," Guard says.

Paul shakes his head. "Won't work. I promise you, I've tried everyth—"

"Bring. Her. Out. Here." Guard repeats. I know that tone. Guard is losing his patience.

"Fine." Paul sighs and moves toward the main door of the studio.

When he's out of earshot, I look over at Guard and say, "Holy Fuck! That girl is unbelievably hot."

Guard laughs loudly. "Glad you think so."

I'm not sure I like the sound of Guard's suddenly lighthearted change of tone. "What? Why?"

But before Guard can answer, Maddie walks out with Paul, stopping dead at the sight of us in full biker gear. Her mouth falls slightly open as her gaze moves between Paul to us and back again.

"A pleasure to meet you Maddie." Guard extends his hand. Maddie hesitates a long moment before finally placing her hand in his. His hand appears to be twice the size of hers. Maddie immediately lifts her chin in a decree of silent strength. "Maddie, it seems we have a little problem. My gorgeous, pregnant wife wants you to sing at our anniversary concert. Your brother here tells us this is an issue for you. I'm hoping we can come up with some solution to that issue."

"Um…" She looks from Guard to me and back to Guard again. "I don't do many concerts." She starts to back up.

Her attempt to cut the conversation short and retreat to the studio is interrupted by Paul's request. "Maddie, hear them out."

I am completely entranced by Maddie, sensing her inner fight. Having seen the news coverage of her abduction, I feel a deep need to protect Maddie. I have to taper the need to pull Guard aside, knowing this would be completely disrespectful to the president of my MC and brotherhood.

"Tell me why you won't perform," Guard persists, frustration setting his jaw.

"I prefer to record only." Her voice is soft and sweet; musical just like her. She fidgets with her hands, wringing them together yet defiantly keeping her chin up.

"You're not telling me why." Guard says firmly, though I can tell he's trying to maintain a softness in his voice to not upset her.

"I just don't think it would be a good idea," she replies firmly. "I'm better in the studio, leaving the stage shows to Paul and the guys. They're better at it."

"No offense to your brother, but my wife wants you," Guard tries again. "I feel like you're still not telling me why."

Maddie's eyes flit from Guard to myself before landing on her brother. "I don't want to do this," she says, shaking her head. "I don't even want to be having this conversation."

"I swear to you, Maddie, you would never be left unattended," Paul promises. "The shit from before—that will never happen to you again."

Maddie crosses her arms in front of her, almost like a shield. "You can't make those promises." Her voice is a hissing whisper.

"What if I give you your own personal body guard from the time you drive into the parking lot and I will have him take you home afterward? He will make damn sure that no one comes within reaching distance of you." Guard can be very persuasive. "I want my wife to be happy. This is the only thing she wants for our anniversary. You can understand that, can't you Maddie?"

Maddie continues to wring her hands together in frustration. "I do understand, and I think it's great that you want to make your wife happy, but I'm still not sure about this." Her eyes hold a tremendous amount of concern.

"You'll have my fiercest man by your side until you get home. My word—you'll be safe."

Paul pipes up. "Maddie, think about what an opportunity this is for the group." He turns his head to Guard. "Guard will give you his best."

"In fact, you're already looking at my best." Guard motions over to me with a nod. And now I understand his teasing tone earlier.

Maddie's face turns toward my six-foot-three-inch frame. She'd been avoiding eye contact with me before, but now solidly meets my gaze.

"You doubt he can protect you?" asks Guard.

"Um...no. I guess not." Maddie replies hesitantly.

"Any problem taking this on, War?" Guard faces me, looking for the answer he already knows he's going to get. Our friendship goes way back. He is secure in knowing that I would do anything for him.

"No problem," I say simply, still staring at a very agitated Maddie. I make the decision right there, in that moment, that nothing will ever terrify Maddie again.

"Okay, then we're done here. I'm going to make my wife's day." Guard looks at Maddie and smiles. "Thank you for making me a hero with my old lady."

"Looking forward to protecting you, Kitten," I utter as Guard turns away.

Maddie opens her mouth but doesn't say a word.

CHAPTER 2
The Pick Up

War

It has been three weeks since we approached Maddie, leaving her stunned. I am sure she feels she was sledgehammered into performing at an anniversary party for a bunch of rough bikers and their posse. I am sure she had replayed the conversation in her head over and over again. She never actually agreed to anything. And yet, I was informed by Paul that she's arranging the lineup of songs and running through the stage setups. Whether she agreed to the gig or not, Maddie wants the music to be fresh and solid. Paul says that Maddie prides herself on putting on a performance to be remembered.

I learned quite a bit from her brother; forever a perfectionist, Maddie has always been methodical and purposeful when putting together a kickass performance.

Despite her recently developed stage fright, The Smoking Guns are continuing to gain in popularity, and Maddie knows that it has a lot to do with the quality of the music and ensuring concert-goers have an experience like no other.

No one would guess that "stage Maddie" and "everyday Maddie" were one and the same. It's as if a totally different person emerges when the lights are flashing, the stage makeup serving as her mask, the applause her incentive to keep playing and singing.

But according to Paul, it's definitely getting harder. Even prior to the abduction, she has never really been caught up by the insanity of it all. This uphill battle has been getting harder and harder. Paul says that Maddie doesn't want to think about the past or talk about it—with anyone. It's something the rest of the band is learning to live with, even if it's unhappily.

I watched an interview from a couple of years back. They have the entire segment with the interviewer and Maddie sitting on her sofa with her knees to her chest, drinking a camomile tea and chatting. She talks about her brother, Paul. She tells the world that he's so talented as their lead guitarist. She talks about growing up in Tulsa, Oklahoma, and how they'd both dreamed of leaving. What I learn from a deep search off the grid revealed an unhappier start. Their parents had been dead-set against any kind of music career, believing music was an immature dream. There were horrible fights, some had even turned physical, until Maddie turned seventeen. The arguments went from bad to worse; the words were becoming more heated. It wasn't long before fists were flying, her brother took yet another beating, but refused to retaliate against his own father. Paul pulled Maddie into his beat-up jalopy that night and they finally left to pursue their music dream. They spent years working on making amends and now, managed to go home for major holidays, avoiding the topic of career and music all together. I think it's all for show. They want to give the appearance they had a happy childhood. Their parents would never want it to get out that they abused their kids.

In the interview, Maddie went on to say that since two people didn't make a band, she and Paul had actively looked for a bass guitarist, keyboard player, and drummer. Through open mic nights at a club, they eventually met Darren, Troy, and Alex, and soon, their band was complete. So began the glory of the Smoking Guns. She spoke about how she self-taught herself how to play each of the instruments and with the help of her bandmates, she was getting better and better. But her voice and her ability to write lyrics were her real passion and contribution to the group. They released a few songs and it wasn't long before they had a following.

This heart to heart with Paul has been enlightening. We walk to Maddie's door and I rap solidly on it. I can hear the pitter patter of her feet making their way to us. Paul aligns himself to the peephole, obviously a routine. I can see she is appeased when the door swings open. She immediately casts her gaze to Paul's sandy brown hair and deep brown eyes.

"Hi," Maddie says, as the door opens wider, she sees me standing right behind Paul, looking noticeably surprised.

"Hey, sis, you ready?" Paul takes a step in and Maddie watches as Paul and I waltz right into her apartment. I notice how compact the place is, or maybe it's because my frame just enhances it smallness.

"Hey Maddie." I say, looking deeply into her eyes as I flash a smile her way.

Maddie looks up at her one-man protection team and settles her shoulders before innocently sending a half-smile my way. She seems calm and relaxed. Maybe because of my large rugged frame or my *don't mess with me attitude*, she feels safe. It could be that she senses my confidence. Or it could just be that I'm being calm.

I can see the flash of calm disappears and I can almost read her mind. She's probably wondering, *but can I really trust anyone?*

I tower over Maddie. My huge arms would probably engulf her. I'm not stupid and I've had my fair share of women who comment on my looks. They seem to have a thing for my dark wavy hair that curls around the nape of my neck when I'm too lazy to go get it cut like now. The leather jacket and t-shirt just magnify the largeness of my body. I maintain myself and strive to always be at my fittest.

"Hi," she says, avoiding my eyes. Instead, she looks down at my deep tanned motorcycle boots, then turns to Paul and asks, "Where is everyone else?"

"In the van. You ready?" Paul replies.

"Yes. Let's go. We have a couple of hours to do sound check and a quick run through." A certain confidence always seems to arise when Maddie talks business. I lift my brow, thoroughly amused.

"Get your stuff. Let's move." I rumble. Maddie hops at the sound of my deep voice as it vibrates through the room.

Exiting onto the curb, Maddie eyes the van and starts to walk over to it. I stop her with a firm hand, grasping her upper arm. She turns her head to see me holding onto her.

"You're with me," I tell her.

"Umm, I can go—" Maddie begins but I don't give her the opportunity to finish her thought.

"I'm responsible for your protection, so you come with me." I am dead serious, leaving her looking a little shell shocked as she stared into my eyes. She stares for a minute and then looks at Paul and the van.

"Meet you there, sis," Paul says, being no help at all to her pleading face. "We'll be right behind you."

Allowing herself to be led away, Maddie finds herself in view of my Harley. "I've never been on a bike," she says softly.

"Not a problem. All you have to do is hold on." I climb on and direct her. "Take my hand." Maddie looks at my hand and cautiously slides hers into mine. This is the first time I've had the opportunity to touch her and something as simple as our hands connecting sends an electrical current through me. I distract myself by checking to make sure her helmet is on safely. "You're safe. I won't go fast or try to freak you out, okay?""

"Okay." She is still tense but lets out a small sigh.

"You need to hold on," I instruct her.

"To what?" she asks as she lifts her shoulders in question.

I turn my head over my shoulder and smile. "To me. Wrap your arms around me."

She hesitates, I take the liberty to tug gently on her arms and pull her closer, wrapping her arms around my waist. Now she is firmly nestled with her front to my back, our thighs melded together, her arms around my abs.

I fire up the bike. "Don't let go, Kitten." Easing into the ride, I take it slow for her sake.

CHAPTER 3

The Rehearsal

War

Regrettably, I feel Maddie's hands release their grip from my waist. We reach the club, or more accurately, the tents set up along the field behind the club. I watch Maddie carefully. She removes the helmet and returns it to me politely, saying thank you. She then appears to take in the whole scene, watching the members and prospects bustling about getting things ready, though she doesn't say a word.

I notice Paul backing up the van next to the stage. Maddie makes a move toward Paul and once again, I take her arm in my vice-like grip. "Maddie, you don't move without me." I look down at her stunned face. Her wide-eyed expression of confusion is adorably cute, makes me want to kiss her so badly. I hold back with great restraint.

"I need to go help unload," she murmurs quietly. Her eyes move toward her band mates, ready to take off as soon as I let go. "We're a team. We do this together," she said more sternly.

Is she kidding? No way can she carry any of that equipment. Demon is standing near the tent and I call him over.

"Get some prospects to help unload and setup the band's equipment. I'm taking Maddie to the tent. When the guys are ready, send someone over." I look down at Maddie, still staring at me and looking a little irate at my taking over. "All set. Let's get you out of view so these boys can focus on setup and not your pretty face."

I tag her hand and lead her to the tent.

Catering to Maddie's concern about security, Guard had this tent setup right next to the stage with everything the band might need available to them.

"Kitten, you ever going to say more than two words to me at a time?" I try to make conversation, get her to open up to me a little. This patience crap is difficult for me. I just want to let her know how this is going to go from now on. Tell her she will always be protected because I won't have it any other way.

"What do you want me to say?" she asks carefully, looking up at me.

"Anything you want to ask me?" I smile. "You aren't curious at all?"

"Why do they call you War?" Her voice is quiet and she tilts her head to the side as she asks. It's a simple question but has a dramatic history I'd rather not divulge at this point. I want her to feel safe and secure around me, not want to run off.

"A while back, when we all settled here and made this our home, some rival clubs decided they were going to make our lives difficult. We held out and never backed down and I was put into some nasty situations—always came out ahead though. I would go to war for my brothers and told them that. When I got patched, Guard called me War." I give the PG rated version of the story, and I still think I worry her. She's biting her lower lip again. "My turn. Why do you hate the stage?"

"I didn't know I had to answer questions." She smiles shyly with a glint of daring and teasing in her tone.

I take in her smile, reveling in the change of demeanour. She almost looks relaxed.

"Fair is fair." I say and smile back.

She lets out a sigh and turns away from me. "A few years back, someone stormed the stage. He had a knife and held it to my neck before forcing me to go with him. I can't remember much more. I blocked stuff out. I do remember his voice and the threats of what he was going to do to me." She's visibly shaking.

I want to find this fucker and kill him with my bare hands, slowly and painfully. I walk behind her, put my hands on her shoulders, pulling her back, and gently say, "No one gets near you. I swear. I would have to be dead for anyone to get within five feet of you." I am so close I can smell her. Vanilla and strawberries. Fuck! I want this woman and I can't do this the way I know how. Gentle does not describe me. I'm not even sure I can do gentle.

She turns around to face me and puts her hand on my forearm. "Thank you. I do feel better knowing that you're here. I know it must be no fun playing babysitter." Her head is on my heart and I swear she can hear it pounding. I wrap my arms around her shoulders and relish the moment.

"Am I interrupting?" Guard is standing at the entrance of the tent. I can see he's stunned by the sight of Maddie wrapped up in me. "I just wanted to check that you have everything you need."

Maddie jolts back, but I hang on to her and keep her loosely at my side. "We're fine."

The entire entourage of The Smoking Guns enter the tent, all staring at me and my arm around Maddie. They look confused and the girls have their mouths hanging open. Again, Maddie shifts to move away from me. I know it's because people are staring, not because she wanted to move. I hang on tight. I don't want to lose contact and I love the way her body fits into mine.

"We should start getting ready." She looks at Paul and he nods but doesn't actually say anything. Maddie clears her throat, trying to get back control of the situation. "Is the stage set?"

"Yeah. I think we should get dressed first and then try the sound." And with that, Maddie chameleons into an assured persona.

"Okay, Brianna and Michelle, let's unpack the make-up and get moving," Maddie commanded. Wow! All fucking business. Who is this woman? The mere mention of music and she turns into the confidence queen.

"Sure," one girl said while the other nods. No idea who is who at this point. Although they're both lookers, they don't hold a candle to the attraction I feel to Maddie.

"Guys, get out. We need to get changed. Paul, can you guys have a dozen water bottles just off-stage? I want to make sure we stay hydrated."

And the direct, all-business attitude continues to roll.

"Sure, sis." Paul turns to Darren, Troy, and Alex. "Let's give them some space."

"We'll be ready in half an hour and then meet you on stage." Maddie moves to where a mirror and table are setup on one side of the tent.

Everyone but the girls file out. "Maddie, I'm standing just outside the door. You yell if you need me," I assure her.

Maddie lifts her eyes to me and quietly says, "Thank you."

Guard is waiting for me just outside the tent flap. The attack starts as the moment I walk out. "What the hell is going on between you two?" he growls.

"Nothing yet," I reply calmly.

"I promised her she was going to be safe. Watch yourself, War. She's off limits," he commands.

"She *is* safe," I counter loudly. And then add in a much lower, more deliberate tone, "She is mine. I want her." And with that statement said out loud, I know my life was changing fast. I have never given any woman the title of being mine.

"Have you lost your fucking mind?!" Guard retorts. I've clearly pissed off our president.

"Before you go all ballistic on me, did anything stop you from getting with Ava?" I counter. I dig into the fact that he was so far gone over his wife that nothing she said, nor any barrier she put up deterred him from being with her.

"Jesus! That was completely different." Guard rubs a hand over the back of his neck.

"I'm not going to do anything until tonight is over. My job is to stay close and keep her safe. No one gets near Maddie tonight," I say. "Tomorrow I work out a plan to keep her with me."

He looks shocked. "You're out of your mind," shaking his head.

"Maybe. But I've been loyal and have never asked for anything. You ask, or the crew asks, and I give. Now I'm asking; I want Maddie. You with me?" I ask. I'm blunt, but I want this woman. I have shown loyalty over and over. "I plan on talking with her about this damn soon, so I want this settled now."

"Fuck! If you can get her, then yeah, I'm with you. But you do not cause any problems with the band or the club, and don't freak her out."

"Well, I might unintentionally freak her out. Some shit happened and she's completely on guard." I smiled then added, "But I like a challenge. And I always get what I want."

Guard slaps me on the back. "Wait until the guys hear about this." He lets up and gives me smile that says, *you're completely screwed.*

Guard was right; the guys are going to have a field day with this. I swore never to take a woman permanently and here I am plotting to make Maddie mine forever.

After the stage is lit and the equipment is all setup, Maddie, Brianna, and Michelle exit the tent and walk onto the stage. Maddie is wearing black leather shorts and a red Harley t-shirt with rebel rocker written on the back. She has black leather bands around her forearms with chrome detailing. Holy hell! This is going to be a long night. I stand in front of the stage, watching them work.

"Guys, all tuned up?" Maddie asks matter-of-factly.

"Yeah," come three separate responses.

"Jimmy, we are going to do a run through. You ready with the lighting?" she asks.

"Ready when you are," Jimmy says, beaming a smile her way.

Paul takes the lead. "Let's do *Road Rebel*." He turns to Maddie. "Let's work this song fierce, real rocker chick. Play to the audience. We need to grab and hold them for two hours and keep them wanting more. Counting it off on three."

It was one of their hits, a hard, fast, soulful song about a man who walks out on life and rides the road, searching for a reason to believe again. Maddie sings and I listen wide-eyed and stupid, breathing in the life she exudes with her voice. Her movements on stage mimic the story of deceit and torture and how one woman makes his dark life light again.

The Smoking Guns perform one more song, moving from rock to soul. Sounds like she can sing it all. Maddie blends in sync with the other girls when she's not lead in the song, allowing everyone in the group their deserved spotlight, until it's her turn once again. When she moves back to center stage, she is sexy and smooth. She's nothing like the Maddie who clung to me on my bike. This Maddie is a vixen capable of drawing you into her world with song.

By the time the sound check is done, a small crowd has gathered around the stage. The final line of the song says, "Who's coming home with me tonight? Is. It. You?" There are whistles and applause, but Maddie just smiles and takes three steps back, moving closer to her brother. Paul notices right away and puts his arm around her. This gesture does not go unnoticed by me. Something went terribly wrong at that concert two years ago and I need to know more.

CHAPTER 4
The Master Plan

War

I't's coming up on nine o'clock. Our brother MCs have arrived and there are plenty of them. Five different clubs and they hold church before the party gets started. Someone will fill me in later. Maddie is my priority right now. I can see the crews filing out, the emblems on their jackets evident. Some of these guys are questionable in moral judgement, but the majority are great men, our allied brothers. Our club is about brotherhood and many of the fellow brothers came running when Ava was in trouble and Guard called for reinforcements.

Ava wants to meet Maddie. Guard, as always, asks me to guide her in.

"Maddie, can I come in?" I ask, standing outside the tent with Ava.

Her soft voice replies, "Um... yeah"

We walk in and Maddie reaches out to take Ava's hand. "Hi Ava," she says.

"How do you know who I am?" Ava asks smiling.

"Well, I've heard nothing but 'my beautiful pregnant wife' from Guard, so I think it's a safe assumption you're the famous Ava," Maddie teases.

"Oh, dear. Guard is a little protective." She giggles, though Ava loves her doting hubby.

"I bet. I hope you enjoy the concert, Ava. I'm sorry I was up in the air about this," Maddie explains.

"I understand. I'd love to chat more after the show if you can. I'm such a huge fan."

"I'm sorry. I actually plan on leaving right after, but if you are ever near the studio, let me know and maybe we can meet up," Maddie offers. "Do you know what you're having?" She points to Ava's belly.

"Yes, but Guard doesn't know yet. I was hoping you can sing something to give him the hint tonight."

"How cool!" Maddie says with excitement. "Whisper it to me."

Ava whispers and Maddie says, "I have just the song," then whispers something back.

"I love it!" Ava is jumping up and down. Well more like bobbing and bouncing with the belly.

"Okay, I'll let the band know at the halfway point."

I can't help but think about how great Maddie will fit in with Ava and Vi, another one of the old ladies. I know that what I'm thinking is crazy, but I need to have this woman. I also need to go gentle, which is going to be the real challenge because it's not me at all. I'm used to getting what I want on my terms.

Paul strides in. "Show time, sis. You ready?" He looks at her, concerned.

"I'm good," she says quietly and not very convincingly.

That's when I pipe up, "Maddie I am going to be right in front while you're on stage. If anything freaks you out, you look right at me. "

Maddie stares up at me and smiles. "Okay."

I walk her to the stage and keep eyes on her until I hit my place at the front. My gaze and hers are completely locked. The Smoking Guns start with some opening chords while Paul announces the band.

"The Smoking Guns are here to rock with you tonight. Let me introduce our crew." Paul went through each band member and the backup singers before announcing Maddie. "And finally, the siren that tempts us all to follow her sound, our soulful diva, Miss Maddie."

Maddie struts on stage with attitude and immediately hits a note to stun the audience into complete silence. She then moves in motion to a set of songs clearly designed to ignite and entice the audience. Men sway and women dance to their sound. Maddie throws her body into every song, dancing to the pop songs, grinding to the hard rock, and swaying to the soft sensual beats.

Fuck, she is beautiful, sexy, and simply amazing. At one point, Maddie says, "This song is for you, Guard, from your lovely wife. I hope you get the clue. I didn't write this, but it is appropriate for this moment." She sings with her brother—*Baby Boy* by Beyoncé and Sean Paul.

All eyes go to Guard as he processes what's happening. He looks at Ava, slightly confused, but when she rubs her belly, he finally gets it. He pulls his wife in for a kiss and the crowd roars.

The place is getting louder and louder, the crowd singing along with the band. Maddie changes her outfits three times, each ensemble more enticing than the one before. The men are drinking hard and I'm hearing some crude remarks about how they want to fuck her into tomorrow, along with some more explicit ways to use her body. It's taking all my strength to not pick them up and throw them across the yard, beating them until they bleed. I can see that Maddie is sensing something too as she's moving back closer to her brother, her eyes hitting mine more and more as the night goes on.

Paul announces the final number, saying, "This is our last one tonight. As always, our beautiful Diva gives a parting gift." He turns to Maddie, "What's it gonna be tonight, gorgeous?"

Maddie takes off her leather choker and brings it to her lips. She lightly kisses the ruby-colored jewel in the center and hands it to Paul. She sings their first hit, *Never Wanted You to Know*. The last note is wavering through the air and the crowd erupts into applause.

After a moment, Paul continues. "Thanks, sugar." He takes the choker and prepares to launch it into the crowd. "Who wants it?"

The crowd erupts. Paul whips it out into the crowd and a sea of hands raise to catch it. "We want to thank you for having us here tonight, and a special thanks to Guard and the Satan's Pride Crew for inviting us to do our thing. Once more with feeling, let me say goodnight on behalf of Darren, Troy, Alex, Brianna, and Michelle. I'm Paul and of course, this is our love-ly Maddie."

I swing myself onto the furthest point on the stage and then follow Maddie off, looking behind me to make sure no one else has the same idea. The band files into the tent. I immediately notice the high everyone is on from the performance. Everyone except Maddie. She is sitting in a chair in front of a mirror, pulling her hair into a ponytail and tying it back. She moves to wipe the heavy makeup until it's clean off her face. Her shoulders are drooped and she places her head in her hands. She looks exhausted.

"Paul," she says calmly. "I need to get changed."

"Yeah. Sure." Paul looked at the guys. "Let's wait outside the tent for a few minutes." They make their way outside.

I don't move. Maddie looks at me. "War, I need to get changed."

"I'm not leaving. They're all riled up out there and I'm not taking a chance of someone coming in." I'm doing this for her protection, but also because I don't want to be away from her.

"I can't change with you here." She said looking at ground.

I turn my back to her. "I won't look."

"You're really not leaving?" I can sense her conflict. She wants me to stay, but she's shy.

"No. Now hurry up and we can make our way out of here."

I can hear her shift out of her clothes, and imagine the jeans shimmying down over her soft, silky hips. I almost groan aloud at the thought. If I close my eyes tight enough, I can see my hands moving over her, licking at her thighs. I'm so hungry for her.

"I'm ready," she calls out, shaking me out of my mental image.

I turn to see her in a soft pink hoodie, faded jeans, and plain converse runners. She looks soft and sweet; a complete transformation from the vixen on the stage. Her eyes are large and she looks like she just wants to go home and snuggle in her bed. Little does she know I want to join her there.

I open the tent flap and tell the rest of the band they can come back in. Guard and Ava make their way in as well.

Ava gushes, "Oh my God, you were fabulous! This was the best present ever!" She hugs Maddie.

Guard pipes up, "I make it happen and she gets the hug?" He loves to tease his old lady.

"Baby, I will thank you properly later. Promise, Honey." She strokes his cheek.

"But seriously, thanks for doing this, Maddie," Guard adds. "I appreciate the special song informing me we're having a boy." I could tell that meant a lot to Guard; he definitely got a little choked up when he heard the song.

"My pleasure," Maddie says, her tone still quiet. "I hate to be a killjoy, but I am bagged. I need to make my way home."

"That might be a problem," Risk says as he enters the tent looking anxious. Risk was only recently patched into club, but he and I are close as brothers come. I know he always has my back. My gaze moves to Maddie and the deep look of concern on her face.

Guard's voice booms. "What's the problem?"

"A bunch of Juries and Relics are out there, fighting over who takes Maddie home tonight." Risk looks concerned. "I have our guys ready but it's gonna get ugly if we move."

The rest of the band falls silent, though it's probably because they're staring at Maddie who goes pale as she wraps her arms around her waist. Paul moves to his sister's side and puts an arm around her.

"Fuck! What the hell is wrong these fuckers?!" Guard explodes, pulling a hand over his face. "This is supposed to be a peaceful celebration. Can you find the heads and leads here tonight?"

"They're spread out. That could take a while," Risk answered.

"Baby," Ava starts, "why can't you just tell them she's got a man? Can't take what's someone else's, right?" Ava looks at Guard and rubs her belly. She knows how to work him—up to a certain point at least. "That way no one gets upset, they all respect the code, and we all move on."

"Angel, first off, that's not how we do things as a club. And second, even if we did, Maddie would have to agree and from there, it only gets more complicated than one little white lie."

"Look, I just want to go home," Maddie says, looking at Guard and then me. "War, you said I was going to be safe."

"Come here, Maddie." I hold out my hand to her. She stares at it for a few seconds before walking over. I pull her to my side. "We need to talk. You and me. Alone." She looks up at me, bewildered. I speak directly to Guard. "I need a minute with Maddie. Could we get some privacy?"

Guard motions everyone outside and tags his wife's hand to lead her out as well. He stops right in front of me and states, "You better be sure, man. This ain't no joke."

Paul looks hesitantly at his sister but leaves when he gets the nod from Maddie letting him know she is good.

"I'm sure."

Guard pulls an inquisitive Ava out the tent.

Maddie watches everyone leave until I pull her around to face me.

"Maddie, we have a couple of options here. One, you let me lay claim to you. That would mean you belong to me. This is no light, bullshit thing. You say yes, and you are mine. Option two, we defend you and get you out of here, even if it may cause some drama with the MCs and create some extra work for Guard in the peace talks that he has been working at for the past few years. Either way I made a promise to protect you and I will."

Maddie's mouth hangs open in shock. She blinks. Closes her mouth then shakes her head. "Lay claim? You don't even know me. I don't know you. What does this even mean?" Her voice starts to shake, and her lips start to tremble. I see she's about to shed tears.

"Calm down, Kitten. Would it be so bad? You need someone to protect you and if you haven't noticed me staring, I think you're beautiful. As a matter of fact, I wanted to lay to claim to you anyway. Of course, I was hoping to give you more time to get to know me first." I take her hands in mine. "Tell me you haven't thought of me since we met." I knew I was pushing her, but we were running out of time and this was the perfect solution as far as I was concerned—I get Maddie and there's no conflict.

"Just because I thought of you doesn't mean anything…" Maddie starts.

"Yeah, it does."

"This is crazy." Maddie's shakes her head. I hold her closer, wrapping my arms around her waist and she automatically places her hands on my chest to push me away.

I won't let her.

"Kitten, you like me. I know you do. You know you do. You're just scared." She lowers her head. "Let me see those pretty eyes." She slides her eyes back up to mine. "I'm gonna kiss you," I say quietly. "We can see if we both like it. Then we can make up our minds."

I have no doubts, but I figure this way she'll feel like she has control over the situation. I tilt her head and hold her still then slowly lower my mouth to hers, licking across her lips. I can feel her stiffen.

"Open your mouth for me, Kitten. Let me taste you." I feel her mouth open slightly and that's when I move my tongue in and pull her fully against me. It takes her a moment to adjust then soften with a barely audible sigh. That's when I feel her kissing me back. Her hands move up from my chest to wrap around my neck. God, she feels good against my body. So soft. So sweet. Her lips are like nectar to a starving man. I slide my tongue deeper into her mouth, enticing hers to duel with mine.

Now that I've tasted her, I can't let her go. She is mine. But I pull back, ending our kiss. I still hold her close and watch as her eyes flutter open. She looks so beautiful, I just want to make her look that way over and over. She looks up at me.

"What do you think, Kitten?" I lower my lips to her cheek and give her soft kisses on her ear.

"I can't think straight when you do that." She breathed out. "What does 'claiming' mean for me?"

I continued to kiss her ear and neck. I can't seem to help myself.

"It means that we're a couple. Together in every way. You'll stay with me and I'll make sure you're cared for and safe. We look after each other." I thought this sounded innocent and sweet enough since I left out my intense desire to undress her and make her moan for hours until we're too exhausted to move.

"I want to make music and record..."

"You can do all that. I'll even build you your own studio at the house, so you can work on your music anytime you want." I continue to move my hands in small circular patterns on her back, keeping her close.

"War, I'm not... I'm not very good with..."

I can see she is struggling with what she wants to tell me. "Kitten, you're safe with me. Just say it." I kiss her lips lightly.

"I haven't been around a lot of guys." I feel her try to twist away from me, but I hold her steady, keeping her with me.

"Baby, look at me." I wait for her to make contact. "I know this is crazy. But we can take it slow." I don't want to lie to her, so I tell it to her straight. "I want you,

Maddie. And I mean to have you in my bed, but I will never hurt you. We can move slowly. Now, that being said, if we go out there," I gesture towards the opening of the tent, "we have to put on a show. I will need you to play along with any touching and kissing and whatever else I think is necessary to get them off our backs."

Risk pops back in. "I don't mean to push you, but things are heating up and the crowd is moving closer and closer to this tent. We got a plan yet?" He looks to me for an answer.

I look at Maddie. "Kitten?"

"I'm scared." She looked it. She's gripping my forearms, her face pale.

"You've gotta trust me. No one gets near you no matter what decision you make," I assure her and pull her close so we're touching.

"Okay, we'll try to be a couple." It's only a whisper and only meant for me.

Fuck, yes! Thank Christ!

I keep my cool and turn to Risk. "Get Guard."

I pull Maddie to my side and wrap my arm around her. Guard, Risk, and the band walk back in.

"Right, so Maddie has agreed to be mine." I say clearly and decisively.

"What the fuck?!" Paul shouts. "No way. Not happening. Maddie come here." He starts to walk over.

Maddie looks at Paul and calmly says, "Stop. Paul, I'm good." She pauses before continuing. "Really, I am. War and I understand each other and this is the best way. I need you to be cool and calm down."

"You don't want him. I know you, Maddie, and you have no clue what'll be expected of you."

"Paul, I'm twenty-nine. I've been through enough to know what I do and don't want. Thank you for being concerned, but I get to make my own decisions." She was smooth, almost cold. "Should I remind you that I didn't want to do this concert in the first place but you insisted? Now you want to tell me who to be with? I can decide that for myself, thanks."

Guard looked stunned, and for that matter, so was I. Showing some serious backbone! This woman never ceases to amaze me.

Guard finally spoke, "Risk, you lead the way. The rest of the band will follow you. I suggest you take them straight to their van. The equipment has already been dismantled and put away. War will walk out with Maddie and Demon close by." Guard's tone changes as he stares right at me. "This has to be real. They gotta know she's yours in every way. Do you understand?"

"Perfectly."

"Maddie, do you get this?" Guard asks her firmly.

"Yes. But how do we make sure it looks real?" So innocent. Jesus, she is going to kill me.

"Follow War's lead. Let him do the talking and do not let go of him." Guard is adamant. He turns back to me. "Keep her close. Fuck, make sure they see you and then find a quiet place and stay for a while before taking her with you. Maybe go upstairs to your room for a while, then duck out the back to get her to her place. You go there together; you stay there together. I don't want any unwelcome surprises should some asshole follow."

"Yeah, right." I answer. And he is right. We have to do this by the book. I turn to Maddie. "You ready, Kitten?"

She holds my hand tighter. "I think so."

CHAPTER 5

Our Beginning

Maddie

Guard leads the way out of the tent ahead of us as War holds me close to his side. I can sense my body tense up and I continue take deep breaths in an attempt to relax as we approach the party zone. War said this party was a reunion of sorts and not as wild as their normal parties.

The clans are spread out throughout the property. I feel War pull me even closer as we enter the main area.

"Show time Kitten. Stay with me." I hear from War's deep sultry voice, just before we get to the loudest section where the music is blaring. Heads start to turn and stare as we make our way closer to the party.

We move around the bar area and War reaches over to grab a shot and downs it with one hand, keeping me firmly in place so that our bodies are touching, and

I can feel the heat radiating, making my senses acute and on high alert. We walk the long way around and War acknowledges his crew with nods or chin lifts and the occasional "hey". I am aware of War becoming very wary as we approach a group in black leather jackets and I can tell immediately that they aren't part of the Satan's Pride MC because their cuts have a very different insignia. I assume this is the herd of possible trouble makers that inspired this "couple make expedition". Without any warning, my back is hauled to the wall. The movement is firm, and I can see that War was taking care not to hurt me. His action is a firm statement that he is staking his claim loud and clear.

"Okay, Kitten, this is it. I am going to pull you into me in twenty seconds and kiss you hard. Pull close and wrap your arms around my neck. You with me?" I shudder in anticipation as his voice rumbles near my ear.

"Yeah." My voice is soft and husky; I barely recognize it. I'm pulled close to him with my body wedged tightly between his body and the wall as his mouth descends over mine, hard. My lips open immediately as his mouth devours mine. I am so shocked by my own response that I cling to him in hopes that this kiss will never end. His hand is fisted tightly in my hair and he tugs my head back as he looks into my eyes. I see the heat in his eyes and without thinking, slide my hands up, one over his shoulder and the other around his neck to pull his head back down. He immediately reacts and takes over in a long, wet breathless kiss as I press my body into his, hoping we find ourselves welded together in this sensual bliss. He plunders my mouth as his hand moves down my back and slides under the pink hoodie to make contact with my bare skin. I am on fire from his touch. He slowly pulls away from our kiss and moves his lips across my cheek as I hear his heavy breath near my ear.

"You taste good. I want more." And with that he nips at my lobe and neck as I try desperately to get my body under control but despite my best effort, my body tremors against his. "My Kitten likes my mouth on her skin. You going to purr for me, Baby?" He says this loud enough for the onlookers but in this moment, I couldn't have cared less and would have openly purred just his have him kiss me like that again. I move my head back and he places his forehead against mine, giving me a chance to catch my breath.

"Hey, you gonna join us here?" I hear the rumbling of Guard's voice coming from the table area.

"Alright, Baby, we are going to walk right past them towards Guard and Ava. You good?" War says as he gives me a light squeeze with his finger on my hips.

"I'm good. Don't let go of me, okay?" I say as he buries his face in my neck. Sweet Jesus! Is he trying to kill me? He smells so good and I can't seem to think straight when I am around him.

"Never letting go." I hear, and in that moment, I really want that to be true. He gently pulls away and takes my hand firmly in his as we make our way over to Guard. War nods to the bikers that have accumulated to watch the "War and Maddie show". I thought it would be smart to gaze adoringly at the magnificent biker beside me and got an affectionate squeeze moving me closer. I leaned into him.

War settles into a chair next to Guard and pulls me onto his lap where I settle snuggly into his body. I feel so comfortable with him; I have never felt this safe with anyone. I remotely hear War and Guard talking about some of the topics at the meeting earlier today while Ava is chats about everything and anything. I'm not paying too much attention, so my responses are limited to nodding and smiling. Truth be told, I'm living in a happy haze, still tasting War on my lips, so much of what Ava is saying isn't sinking in.

After a good half hour, I remembered that my brother had to make it out of here along with the rest of the band. I began wondering if they're okay and before I lose myself in worry I ask, "War, did Paul and the others get to the van ok?"

"I saw them get in. They're fine but we can call them in a while if you want."

"Yes, please."

"You alright, Kitten?"

"I'm wiped." I said, honestly. "I just finished a two-hour show and I am just drained." It has been a day unlike any other and I'm mentally and physically done.

War turns his head to Guard. "Maddie's had enough, and I just want to get the fuck out of here. I'm taking her to my room. Can you get a prospect to guard our entrance?"

"Yeah, and get her out before morning? I want no women here when we have our meeting. I want you here for that. I'll send a prospect to stay with Maddie until you get back." Guard signals to a guy called Cris. He has a jacket patched "prospect" and even I know that means he's a potential new Satan's Pride member.

War lifts me into his arms like I'm light as a feather, "Wrap your arms around my neck, Baby. I'm taking you upstairs to rest." I do as I'm told but can't help myself and kiss his jaw, burrowing my face into his neck to I can take in his scent.

"Sleep sounds good." I mumble.

CHAPTER 6

Sleepovers

War

I lay my beautiful girl down on my bed and she is so exhausted she doesn't fight me when I take off her shoes or when I slide in beside her and envelop her in my arms. One of her arms is draped over my belly and her head is resting on my chest. In her effort to get comfortable she drapes her leg across mine as well. I don't want to move; I can stay like this all night.

I fall asleep listening to her soft breaths, her sliding a hand under my t-shirt. She is safe, and she is mine.

I am alerted by Cris that it's coming up on six a.m. and I need to get Maddie off the premises before the place comes alive. I don't want to move. I have my woman up against me tight with her long flowing hair curled around my chest and arm. Her hoodie rose to settle under her breasts, baring her midriff. Her face is tilted up, so I can see her perfect red lips beckoning and I surrender myself to a taste of heaven.

I lick her lips and am rewarded with a little sigh of contentment. I can feel my pants tighten and swell. I must extract myself and get her out of here before I lose myself in making her give me more of those sighs.

"Kitten, we need to get out of here." I kiss her cheek. I can't help myself.

"Mmm." She moves to bury herself deeper and her hand starts a decent from my chest to my hard bulge. I grab her hand before she gets there, and her eyes flicker open. "Is it morning already?" she says in a groggy mumbled voice.

"Yeah, Baby. We need to get out of here. Get ready." I move myself away from her and make my way to the bathroom to give my dick a few minutes to settle itself.

Maddie is pulling her hair back into a ponytail and slipping on her shoes when she catches my eyes. "Do I have time to run in and splash some water on my face before we go?" Her cheeks are pink, and she looks so sweet biting her lower lip and forcing herself to look right into my eyes.

Two strides and I have her in my arms, lower my head and kiss her softly on the mouth. "Yeah, Baby. Do it quick, though. I wanna get you home."

"Okay," She slips past me. There's a rough knock on the door and an impatient Risk on the other side.

"Need to get you out now," he says. "Ava and Vi are leaving and the rest of the women were gone hours ago. You need to move before Guard loses his shit. Some idiot last night was getting some ideas about tapping your woman last night. Guard had to have a word with his leader. So, you see anyone out there this morning, you grab her and make it known she's yours."

Just then Maddie re-entered the room. She heard it all. I can tell by the look on her face. "I'm ready. She looks at Risk, then at me and takes a deep breath. "Maybe I should go away for a while. I could hide away..." Her voice trails off when she sees my face harden.

"No. You stay with me. You're mine. You and I made that decision last night. You knew there was no going back," I bite out and I'm sure I've scared her when I see her lip quiver. Shit! I don't want to upset her but there's no way I'm letting her out of my sight now that I finally have her with me.

"I don't want anyone getting hurt because of me," she says softly. And it hits me that in that moment she's more concerned for the safety of me and my family than she is for herself.

"Things will die down." I reach for her hand and encased it in mine. "Grab your purse and bag." I lead her toward the back entrance where my bike is waiting for us. Turning to Risk, "Make sure someone is at Maddie's for 9:30 this morning so I can make the meeting. I'll be heading back when it's done."

"Clubs are watching from above man." He smiles and says, "Fuck! They like your girl."

"Kitten, how much do you like me?" I asked calmly.

She moves her mouth close to my ear. "A lot."

"Okay, Baby, show me, or even better, show them." I say, tilting my head toward the windows above.

Maddie moves from standing beside me to getting as close as she can. She moves her hand around my neck into my hair and pulls me down so that our heads and lips are less than an inch apart. I feel her tongue on my lips, tracing the edges and then she bites gently down on my lower lip and tugs. I am completely undone. I jerk her close to drag her mouth to mine. I want to own that mouth. Maddie's lips meet mine and I kiss her back with the same fervour and desire. This is not a kiss. It's an assault. It spins even more out of control when I feel her hands in my hair, tugging me closer into her. My hands roam over her body, settling one on her ass, where I pull her in close and pin her to my body so I can feel every sexy curvy part of her.

"You two want to take that home?" Risk interrupts. "Fuck me! I need to go take a cold shower." He teases.

I break the kiss but keep my Kitten in my arms. "Get on, Baby, and hold tight." I help her on; and groan silently as she slides her arms around my waist. I want to get her home and I want to get her under me. All the good intentions about moving slow are quickly being banished from my thoughts.

CHAPTER 7
Moving Maddie In

Maddie

Despite my best effort to hide my exhaustion, I know it's written all over my face. I'm still reeling from the overnight changes that have occurred in my life. It normally takes me a day to settle back into a regular routine after a performance, but between zealous bikers and a mind-blowing kiss with War, my mind was spinning with emotions buried deep within me, threatening to spill over. I'm doing my best to contain my thoughts and hang onto the hope I feel when he looks deeply into my eyes and I feel like the me I was before the horrible abduction ever happened. As we walk in to the apartment the is phone ringing; I pick up my pace to grab it, knowing that it's probably Paul, worried sick about me.

"Hello?" It's my sweet brother Paul. I'm sure he's feeling guilty. He's also being over-bearing. Up until yesterday that never bothered me and I would either simply ignore his behaviour or relish in it because I know it comes from of a place of love and protection.

I do my best to placate him, but he's harping now, and I am beginning to lose my temper. I was always the quieter child, and very rarely put up a fuss. Something needed to be very important for me to disagree with him, usually around the music we wrote. That's a fight I always won.

"I'm fine." I listen to his concerned voice and try to reassure him. "Everything is good." He interrupts with more questions and again I tell him that I'm good. "Honest, Paul." Now I'm getting annoyed. "Oh Lord, I'm not a child and I was not coerced." How dare he think I have no mind of my own? "Paul I'm a little insulted you think that I'm not capable of deciding who I do or don't want to spend time with. You were furious when I refused to take this gig, then went all out to get me there. Now you want to pull the big brother card and tell me I am getting involved with a scary bunch. You are the one who brought this bunch to the studio."

BIG SILENCE followed by a lighter one-sided chat about how he worries for me. I can feel Paul's doubt through the phone and under normal circumstances would be more understanding of his feelings, however I can see War leaning against the counter of my kitchen and he looks highly amused by the conversation. I become so intrigued with the slight lift of his lips curling into a smile that I almost forget Paul rambling into my ear. I decide it's time I cut him off.

Then in a very determined and cold voice: "I decide my future. What are you afraid of?"

Paul says nothing, but I know he's thinking about that night when everything changed. I am taking back my life. I am going to see where this relationship goes, and I am not going to give up or compromise my singing to do it. Not everything is going to change overnight but I am going to take things one day at a time.

I want to reassure Paul that we will never change. Our band will always be what it is, and he is always going to be the best big brother ever. "I will continue to write and sing because I love it and I need you to be my brother, not my guardian or my business manager. I also need a break. We have been working non-stop and I need one. Badly." I use my soft voice and drop my eyes away from War.

Paul wants me to go on tour with them.

"I never go on tour," I remind him, then continue, "I am being well looked after. GO! Just make sure you all come kiss me goodbye this afternoon."

There is a heavy sigh from the other side of the phone and Paul knows that this isn't a battle he will win.

"See you around two o'clock then. Love you, big brother."

With that I hang up the phone and plop myself on the sofa. "Baby, go take a shower and then you can settle." War says. He's behind the sofa with his hand sifting through my hair.

I looked up at him. "So tired," I say. My eyes feel heavy. It was a long night and my body isn't used to the emotional ass-kicking it got yesterday. War rounds the sofa, kicks off his boots and hauls me closer, snuggling me in beside him. I don't struggle. I don't want to do anything but rest my head in the crook of his shoulder and close my eyes which I do almost immediately. It's been a tough few days. The life I've created for myself is very minimal. I live in my small sanctuary. My apartment is cute and cozy with just me in in it most of the time unless Paul came by. Now I've agreed to forge ahead in a committed relationship to a biker in a motorcycle club. I realize there is so little I know about War. Through the conversation he had with Guard, I picked up that he managed and was part owner of a mechanic shop that specialized in motorcycles and muscle cars shop. I can sense that my life is going to change and only hope that we step through these changes in increments I can handle.

It must be the quiet and the warmth of War's body next to mine that has me drifting off into a peaceful slumber.

I am awoken by gentle hands stroking my hair. "Maddie? Kitten?" I hear the gentle rumble of War's voice. I place my hand over his and War slides his hand down across the apple of my cheek. As I shake the drowsiness, I focus on those beautiful laughing eyes and instantly my heart beats faster.

"Yeah, Honey?" I mumble without steeling my gaze from his.

He says nothing. His face moves over mine and our fingers link together followed by a soft slow kiss. Our mouths connect in a deep, wet kiss. We take our time exploring each other, mouths slanting this way and that, desperately wanting to get even closer.

I open my eyes and out of the corner of my eye notice a Satan's Pride leather jacket filled with arms.

I pull back and whispered against his lips, "Someone is here for you."

War turns his head to see a Satan's Pride prospect at the door. I recognize Cris from the party last night and he is standing in the doorway looking at us, failing to suppress a grin.

"Hey," says Cris.

"Hey." I nod back.

War says, "How much time do I have to get back?"

"Starts in forty-five minutes. I came a little early in case you need me for anything." Cris is a large man—not as big as War, but no slouch. War has commented several times that he is young but loyal. He has done everything the club asked and has shown his allegiance over and over.

War turns towards me, "Baby, go take your shower. I need a few minutes with Cris and then I will come into the bedroom before I go."

I blink and tilt my head to one side. "Everything okay?"

"Absolutely, Kitten. Just want to make sure you're settled before I have to leave for a bit."

"Okay." I make my way into the bedroom. A shower sounds wonderful right about now.

I take my time under the hot cascading water. I lather my hair with rose-scented shampoo and my mind wanders. I think about how much I love the feel of War's hands sifting through my hair, pulling me close and holding me tight. I loved the feel of his hands on my ass and the hardness of his body pressing against mine. I want this, and I want him. I rinse my hair and body and shut off the water, blinking the last of it out of my eyes.

I walk into my bedroom wrapped in a towel, my hair is wet and wild around my face with curls. I let out an "eek" when I noticed War in my bedroom sitting on the side of my bed. He is beautiful. His toned body, his soulful eyes and luscious lips. I know that my eyes are big and wide. My mouth is dry, and I can barely get the words out. "Um, I need another minute."

"I like you just like that." He teases, the corners of his mouth turning upward.

I can feel the heat in my cheeks. Blushing profusely, I say, "Please."

"One minute, Kitten. I have to go and want to talk to you before I head out." He motions for me to come closer. Instead I grab a pair of shorts, a tank, bra, and panties and escape back into the bathroom. I rush to put on my clothes knowing that he is supposed to be leaving and not wanting to delay him from a meeting that seems important. My hair still wet, I re-enter the bedroom. My shorts aren't much coverage and expose too much of my legs and my tank top feels tight against my chest. I can feel my nipples hardening at the sight of him.

"Come here," He asks, crooking his finger my way and motioning for me to stand between his splayed legs. I walk to him and place my hands in his without hesitation.

"Yes." I say, as I'm pulled even closer and positioned to sit on his knee; his fingertips gliding up my back instigate a tingling sensation along their path until his fingers tease a loose tendril of my still damp hair.

"I have to head back. Cris is staying here while I'm gone. I want you to pack some stuff for the next few days. We're heading to my place when the meeting is over. I should be back by 1 p.m. and I will pick up something for us to eat. What do you want, Baby?" He continued to caress my back and placed his other hand on my thigh making tiny circular patterns and edging his hand higher and higher.

"Why are we going to your place?" I say, my breath hitching as War's touch continues to move further and further upward.

"Remember, Baby, we are together. You go where I go. My place is bigger, and you need to know me. We are exploring, right?" He reminds me gently. His hand makes it to the edge of my shorts, which I am now thinking might have been a bad choice. There's little space between his hand and my heat.

"Yes," I say a little breathless. I instinctively reach out to grip his hands a little tighter. I look down to see his expression; he's just as turned on as I am. I bite my lower lip as a quiver moves through my body.

He shifts to guide me off his lap. I don't like losing his closeness. "Pack, Baby. I'll be back very soon." Then he licks my lips and proceeds to tug my lower lip between his teeth and suck on it. I try to resist him with a stifled moan and quickly decide not to resist, enveloping neck with my arms, pulling myself deeper into him. My breasts are up against his hard, firm body and when our lips finally detach, our foreheads touch and our panting breaths intermingle.

"Be a good girl while I'm gone. Want me to pick up something for lunch on my way back?"

"Pizza?" I ask.

"What do you want on it?" he asks as he places wet kisses on my neck.

"Um... I can't think when you do that," I share. Then spontaneously continue, "No pineapple."

"No pineapple. Anything else?" He allows his assault to expand to my collarbone.

"No, I don't think so." I lean back to give greater access to my skin.

"Baby, if I don't stop now, we are both going to wind up in your bed fucking until we both can't move anymore," he informed me.

I take a deep breath and force some space between us. I am led back to the living room where Cris is sitting on the sofa.

"Cris, nothing happens to Maddie." War says. He then turns to me. "Pack for at least a week. I'll be back soon." One shorter hard kiss that still incites me to pull him back to me. I look forward to spending some time with War at his place.

I'm moving in, at least for a little while.

CHAPTER 8

The Move

War

I chose not to inform Maddie that this was going to be the last time she stayed at her apartment. I figure we'll get the rest of her stuff packed and moved in in the next week.

I arrive at the club with fifteen minutes to spare and am confronted by Guard as soon as I walk in. He motioned me into his office.

"So, good night?" he asked slyly.

"Good enough." I reply.

"I am going to make the announcement that you are making Maddie your old lady. Any objections?" he asks.

"Why announce it?" I counter. I don't care that my club brothers know my intentions with Maddie, but I don't think that it's anyone else's business.

"Because when Ava came into my life, I announced it and asked if there was an issue. It's respect for the rest of the club." Guard is set on making sure there are no unforeseen problems in the club and wants everything above board.

"I got no problem with announcing it but why does it have to be when every other club is here?" I want to keep everything low key for Maddie's sake.

"I am making a point here," Guard says in frustration. "Last night could have gone really bad. Getting everyone in our club on board makes for a united front. You wanted me to have your back and I do. Your club has your back too."

"Yeah, I know it does." I start to reply but am stopped.

"Then shut the fuck up and let us make it known that Maddie is untouchable to anyone but you," Guard states firmly.

He has never steered me wrong and I've got to trust that this is the right thing to do. I nod, and we make our way back into the common area where all five clubs from surrounding areas are holed up waiting for Guard to start.

Guard goes through a list of topics and gets input from the other clubs on the business side of things. We talk about the ways we can help one another and where each of us draws the line. We are all pretty much in sync and Guard has worked diligently to see that our clubs work together in peace. He's a great leader and Orion, who has been his right hand since I've been around, is a huge grounding force for our club. Orion stays silent most of the time but has his ear to the ground and knows what's happening before anyone else.

We are close to shutting things down when Guard says, "Since we're here, and I know War wants to make it official, he wants to make Maddie his old lady. I have no objections to this and am asking our club members if there are any concerns."

He looks around the room to rumblings of, "about time you took a woman" and "fuck, you lucked out". Guard moves to close the meeting and hears from a Rebel clan leader, "I can understand why you want her, but she comes with baggage. She could be more trouble than you need. Heard about her stalker. You want that shit in your club?"

I walked to the middle of the room, completely pissed that they think I'd back down because of some idiot teenager with a crush on my woman. "I think I can handle any trouble."

Then Risk pipes up, "Maddie is one of us. We all take responsibility to keep her safe."

Demon slams his hand on the table and nods his acceptance and Guard says, "Maddie is ours and if a devoted member wants this woman, we make room for her."

End of that discussion, thank fuck!

I can't get myself out of there fast enough and at this point its past noon. I call in for the pizza to be delivered to Maddie's and say my farewells. The idea of a stalker continuing to pursue Maddie is really bugging me and I asked Orion to investigate further if there is any truth to the rumor. I will talk to Maddie about it, but I don't want to spook her into thinking that she's in jeopardy. She retreats into herself enough as it is, and I am trying to get her to come out and live life again.

I unlock the front door with the extra key Maddie mentioned on my way out, to find Cris is parked on the sofa with a can of soda in his hand, watching Maddie on the other side of the room strumming her guitar. She is a sight to see. Her lips press together humming a melody and plucking at the strings with her eyes shut as she sways back and forth to the tempo. She stops to make notes on the music sheet on the side table. I stay quiet admiring the sight myself. Cris notices that I've returned and gets up to come over. Maddie is still oblivious to the both of us.

"She's been doing that since you left." Cris states as he drops the can on the counter.

"Yeah?"

"Totally zoned out right after she picked up the guitar. Like she isn't even in this world." Cris shakes his head.

We both turn as she starts to strum again adding lyrics that pull me deep into her.

My world started when you found me
You show me light
Together we take flight
Don't walk away and turn my light dark
Then she continued to hum once again.

"Fuck." Cris whispered beside me. "She's like a magnet. Sucks you right in."

"I know brother. I am living it," I admit. I look at Cris and continue, "Guard will fill you in when you get back. We are heading to my place later this afternoon. I called Molly in town to have groceries delivered to the house, can you meet her at three o'clock?"

Without a pause, "Yeah, sure. Whatever you need." He turns to the door, "I'm heading back. Good luck, man. I have a feeling you have your work cut out for you."

"Right," I say in a low voice.

Once the door closes, I walk over to my girl. "Hey, Baby, I'm back." I'm rewarded with a bright smile.

"Where's my pizza?" she asks with a glint in her eye.

"Where's my hello kiss?" I retorted.

She puts down the guitar on the floor next to her and makes her way to me. She stands on her toes and kisses me lightly on the lips. "Now where is my pizza?" she teases.

"Pizza kisses are with tongue," I taunt.

"Oh, let me try again." She moves back to her toes and sinks one hand into my hair and the other on my shoulder to steady herself. Then I feel the heat of her mouth and glide her tongue into mine. I instantly band my arms around her waist and pull her so that our bodies at touching from chest to thighs. I plunder her mouth like a starving man who hasn't had a meal in weeks. I lick, nibble and duel with her tongue. I don't want to break our connection and I know that Maddie is trying to get closer when her fingers tighten in my hair. I can feel her nipples straining against my t-chest; even through our clothes I can feel her heat.

The doorbell pulls us both out of our cloud. "Pizza's here," I tell her.

She giggles. It's the sweetest sound I have ever heard. I untangle myself from her arms, kissing her lightly on the forehead before heading to the door to get our pizza.

We eat and wait for Paul to arrive. The sooner we have this conversation, the sooner I can get her on my bike to head home. It's nice to see Maddie relax. She chats and nibbles her food. I ask her about her folks and how she got into music. She shares freely and talks about her brother defending her from their parents and their views.

Paul arrives with the rest of his band in tow.

"Hey little Diva." Paul chimes as he walks in, kissing his sister's cheek.

"Hi Paul." She kisses her brother back then turns to the rest of them. "Hi, guys."

"You okay Maddie?" Paul says, sounding concerned as he wrapped his arm around his sister.

I notice Darrin, Troy, Alex, Brianna and Michelle all hang back making themselves comfortable on the kitchen stools and counters. They seem a little intimidated to join me in the living area. However, Troy does ask, "Maddie you sure everything is okay? If you need us just say so. We all have your back."

"Thanks Troy, but I'm good. War is taking good care of me. You don't have to worry while you're on tour because I have my own personal warrior." Then she laughs. I note by the stunned looks on their faces that this is something that rarely happens.

"We'll be gone for eight weeks. I have a list of places we're going to be. You have all our cells. If you want the studio I need to make some calls to reserve time, so just let me know." Paul is running through his checklist still constantly looking at Maddie searching for warning signs that there might be a problem.

"She is getting her own studio." I pipe up.

"What?" Paul asks but all eyes turn to me, including Maddie's.

"It's being designed and added. You guys won't have to worry about studio time from now on. You just come and do your thing. I want Maddie to be able to do what she wants when she wants."

"Are you for real? Do you know how much that's gonna run?" Paul continues to stare.

"Don't care. It's done."

I can hear the side stage mumble, "Fuck." "Are you shitting me?" "Unbelievable." And the one that makes me laugh, "I have to get myself a Satan's Pride member."

Alex reminds them all, "We have to hit the road if we want to get there in time, Paul."

I could see that Maddie's brother is struggling to leave her.

"Go Paul. I. am. fine." Maddie says confidently, smiling at him.

"I got her Paul. Go do what you got to do. Call her every night so she doesn't worry." I get closer to Maddie and stretch out my hand and she takes it, making her way to my side where I wrap her in my arms.

"Okay, but I have to tell you I'm freaked out by this." Paul says waving his arms at me and Maddie.

"We didn't plan it, but it works. We're both happy with each other. The situation has moved things along a little faster than usual, but I swear that she is always going to feel safe. She is my priority. Her happiness is important to me."

He nods to me and I give him a chin lift back.

"I love you Maddie" he says and kisses her cheek. "I'll call you every day to check in."

Maddie puts her hands on either side of his face and kisses his cheeks. "Love you too, big brother. You better call me."

Goodbyes are finally done and although Maddie sheds a few tears, she assures me she's good and snuggles deeper into my arms. I want to get her to my place so we can find our own new rhythm.

"Baby, where are your bags?" I keep my tone light.

"In the bedroom."

"I'll go get them." I move to her room. It's soft and sweet. Robin blue walls with a white wrought iron bed covered in a pink and blue comforter in a simple swirl pattern. Her shelves hold CDs, movies, and books, all neatly stacked. My Kitten made her nest in this room. I wonder how she is going to fare in my home.

I come out to find Cris waiting at the door. "Grab a bag, let's get moving." I say.

Cris and I loaded the car he brought with him because women pack far too much shit and I want Maddie to be able to ride comfortably on my bike with me.

"Baby, what did you pack? No way this is only clothes," I grunt.

"Um, well, I have tons of my music on my iPod and phone, but I also brought some of my favourite CDs and some books, and sheet music that I have been working on. I need to get my guitar." Her voice starts to fade, and she looks away.

"Hey, I was just teasing Kitten. Bring the whole place with you." I'm planning on having her apartment emptied any way. I kiss her on the forehead. "I'll see how we can get more of your favourites later." I whisper in her hair. I want Maddie to feel comfortable and know that I want her with me.

She lifts her eyes and smiles. She's good to go and so am I.

CHAPTER 9

Best Morning Ever

Maddie

Settling in War's kitchen, chopping vegetables alongside my warrior is the most relaxed I have felt in years. I can feel War is completely comfortable in his kitchen chopping red peppers like he does this every day.

I must admit, I was fairly quiet and tense when we first made our way into the house. He walked me through the main living room, showed me the kitchen, which was remarkable for a man's place, and walked through to the den. It wasn't until I was led the spare bedrooms and finally the master bedroom that I noticed how tense I was becoming.

The entire home is a rustic style with leather sofas, a big screen television, and state of the art appliances because Ava insists on the best for when she and Guard are invited over. The bathrooms are all modern as well, with chrome accessories and cream and tan walls.

When he showed me the master bedroom, all I could see was the huge bed and all I could picture was War and me, wrapped up in each other in that bed. War left my bags in the bedroom and told me that there was plenty of time to put things away later. He searched my face and obviously saw that I was freaking out. I had thought all sensuality was abolished from my mind, body, and soul. I've been so removed and avoided intimacy. The only person I've been willing to let put their arms around me has been my brother. I've gotten more and more comfortable with the guys but still avoid even the most casual touch.

War led me back out and down the hallway into the living room. "What's bothering you, Kitten?" He asks, enveloping my hands with his.

"Nothing." I say, not even able to raise my eyes.

With supreme gentleness and patience War asks again. "Baby, I think you're lying to me. I thought we were going to be honest." War places his hand under my chin and raises it so that I can look into those mesmerizing eyes.

I take a deep breath. This is a leap of faith. I want to be with him and that means I need to learn to communicate better. "I'm not used to staying with someone. I haven't ... I don't have..." I stop, and I'm so very embarrassed, I can feel my skin turning scarlet pink.

"Baby, maybe we should talk about your experiences. Not in detail, but what you're comfortable with." He sits down and pulls me along to sit beside him. "Have you had sex before?"

KILL ME NOW!!!!

Something just snaps. Some asshole shook my life apart years ago and I allowed this to happen. I have been living like a nun because I'm too terrified to let anyone near me for fear of losing all I can control. I have very little to lose because I have not taken the time to accumulate friends and memories.

I jump to my feet, placing my hands on my hips.

"War, I was a normal person before the attack. I dated. Although I haven't had many boyfriends thanks to tour life. Yes, I've had sex. But I haven't lived the life that you have, and I think you are going to find me plain. I haven't done much; I'm not some kinky, sexy girl." Then the reality hit, and it just spurted out of my mouth, "What if there are things you won't like about me?" Tears well and my bottom lip starts quivering. "Maybe you should take me back to my place and..."

"NO." He growls it loudly, shutting me up immediately. War rises to stand in front of me, taking a hold of me with one hand while gently caressing my cheek with the other. "What won't I like? So far, I like everything about you." I search his face; he seems so certain and so sincere.

"I have nightmares. I wake up screaming, even after two years, I still can't stop them." I tell him quietly.

"So, I hold you and we talk through it until you fall back to sleep. What else?"

"I get an idea for a song and I get up and start to play the guitar and hum," I say, biting my lower lip automatically.

"I like your music. I find it calming. I can come down and lay on the sofa and sleep here next to you.

What else?" He systematically breaks down every obstacle I utter.

"What if I can't make you happy? I'm not an innocent, but I'm also not as experienced as you." I try to shift back, trying to create distance between us.

"Oh no," he says, pulling me close enough to wrap his arms around my waist as I place my hands on his chest and look up at him. "I don't care about what you think you know or don't know about sex. I know that we want each other. I want you, but I can go slow. I want you to be you." Then he kisses me softly, deeply with purpose. I can feel his desire pressed up against me and I just wanted to hang onto to this moment. When he pulls his head back, I stifle a whimper at the lost connection.

"Did you like that?" he asks, still holding my head and nipping at my lips.

"Yes" I whisper breathlessly. I'm so tempted to drag my hands through his hair and fist them tightly in it to pull his mouth back onto mine.

War has other ideas and falls backwards to lay on the sofa, settling me so that I'm lying on top of him, feeling all the strength and hardness of his body. A strong hand is secure at my waist while the other trails my back with his fingertips. "Kitten, feel me. I am burning for you. I am so hard I can barely control myself." He proceeds to move his hips, so I can feel his erection. "Does this not show you how much I desire you? I want you here with me."

I wiggle upward and position myself so my brow rests on his. "I want you too. I just don't want you to be disappointed."

"Highly unlikely, Kitten. Let's just take one day at a time."

I relax and snuggle to burrow myself securely against his hard body.

"Baby, ten minutes and then we have to start dinner,"," he says.

I let out an audible sigh while moving the tips of my fingers under his shirt loving the feel of his skin.

War

Christ! I don't think I can move slow. Everything Maddie does turns me on.

Maddie is wearing shorts and a tank top, chopping vegetables and bouncing to the beat of the music in the background. She hums and sings with her hair swaying, pretty lips moving and her bright blue eyes gleaming with joy.

All I can think about is how badly I want to set her down on the counter, strip down to nothing, and taste her until she screams. I want to touch her, consume her, and fuck her until I can't move.

"Is the chicken ready yet?"

"Almost. You hungry, Kitten?"

"Starving!" she proclaims.

"Can you wait another fifteen minutes?" I ask.

"I can wait." Then she shyly asks, "Can I ask you something?"

"Anything."

"What's your real name?" Her eyes jut from her hands to my face.

"Xander Cole," I say plainly.

"That's a beautiful name," she says. "It suits you. You look like a Xander."

I start to laugh. "What does a Xander look like?"

She giggles, "Like you. Strong, smart, and hot."

I quirk my eyebrow. "Hot, huh? Good to know you like what you see." I like to tease her. Obviously, I succeed as I notice her face flush. She turns to set the table.

I am wiped and never got caught up on sleep between the concert and running back and forth to Maddie's place. After our late dinner, I lead Maddie to our bedroom. "Why don't you get ready for bed while I make sure everything is shut up tight?"

"Okay." I can see her reach for her bags as I walk out. I think giving her time and space to get comfortable in the room without me might help her get settled. I take the time to lock things down, the exercise of it also giving me time to walk off the lust that's threatening to unleash itself.

The sexiest sight I've ever seen is Maddie in my bed. Her hair is hanging loose, splayed out on the pillow, causing me to get an instant hard on. She's wearing baby pink PJ shorts and a matching tank top. I take off my shirt and walk into the bathroom to cool down. I throw some water on my face, trying not to think about those gorgeous legs and soft mouth. I promised myself that I wasn't going to push her tonight. I was going to wrap her in my arms and make her feel safe with me. I decide a cool shower is necessary.

I make my way to the bed with a towel hanging low on my hips and head over to the dresser to throw on a pair of boxers that I wouldn't have bothered with if I were alone. Then I draw back the covers and ease myself into the center of the bed, nestling Maddie closer and enveloping her in my arms. She quickly adjusts her legs to curl into mine. I take her mouth. I want to taste her again and again. Her lips move against mine with as much need as my own. I pull her underneath me and allow my hand to drift lazily across her breast, flicking the nipple to gauge her reaction. I'm rewarded with a low moan. Shit! I need to stop before I take this further than I planned tonight. I want her to feel safe with me, get her used to me holding her, and touching her. She makes it so damn hard to slow down. Just one more kiss, I promise myself. I drop my mouth to her soft lips and plunge deeper into her mouth, tangling our tongues together. I weave my hand into her hair and grip her curls holding her head steady and feeling the softness caressing my skin. I break away when I know I'm about to lose control and bury myself inside her.

"Baby, I can lose myself in you. I better stop before I take you further than you're ready for," I whisper against her lips.

Her eyes flutter open and her lips part. She looks thoroughly kissed. I feel her move under me. Restless perhaps. Her hands slide from around my neck to rest on my chest. Maddie hesitates for a moment and then peers up through her lashes.

"What if I don't want to stop?" she asks in a barely-there voice.

"Listen, Kitten, it is taking all my self-control to not strip you and kiss every part of you. I don't want you to regret one thing about what we do together, especially in this bed." I say it, but I'm so tempted to rip off her PJ shorts and drive into her body, giving myself the much-needed relief the cold shower failed to.

Maddie kisses my neck and brushes her cheek against my chest. She continues to wriggle under me and I can tell that her frustration is mounting as well.

"Please, Xander, I need more."

Oh Christ, I am going to come undone. I pull lightly on her hair tangled in my fingers, moving her eyes to meet mine. I brush my lips across hers and tug lightly on her bottom lip as I hear her murmur a soft moan.

"Does my Kitten want to purr? I can make you come, Baby. You want that? I can go nice and slow."

Maddie jerks her hips against mine as she says, "Not slow. Fast. Please." She is panting her words and rubbing against my cock.

"Shh, I got you. Lay back and relax." I kiss her throat as my hand roams across her body, sliding across her breasts.

I move under her tank and lift it, caressing her smooth soft skin. I continue to taste her neck, her lips, licking and nipping. I pull down her bra exposing her nipple and tease with my fingers, rolling the peak. I can feel a tremor run through my precious woman. I close my mouth over it and expose the other nipple, continuing my assault.

God, she tastes so good. I hear her gasp and feel her body arch to press further into me. Her cries begging for more are enough to make my already pained cock more strained.

I give each nipple ample attention. I release her hair and use the arm to prop myself up on my side as

I make my way down to her pussy. I slide my hand into her shorts and under her panties and I find her moist center. Her hand grips my shoulder and a gasp of pleasure consumes my Maddie as I slip into her folds, forcing her legs open. Little circular patterns have her lifting her hips to get closer. Her head moves back and forth on the pillow and I hit her nub over and over. I insert a finger deeper inside and continue with my thumb, driving her to distraction. She feels so tight and I know I'll need to go slow when I finally take her.

I can feel her body tense, reaching for relief. "Let go, Kitten. I got you. Let me make you feel good." I whisper as she gasps and mews for the ultimate relief.

In that moment I pluck a nipple in my mouth and sucked hard, pressing down onto her nub. A cry of ecstasy roars through Maddie and her body convulses with tremors. I wrap her in my arms, holding her tight as her breathing normalizes and her grip on my shoulders ease. I move onto my back and pull Maddie with me to rest tucked into my side with her head on my chest. Maddie buries herself deep.

I gave her a few minutes until I know she has settled and tilt her head up to meet my face.

"Baby, you good?" I asked gently.

"Good," she replies in a whisper. Her face is flushed, and I can see the pink in her cheeks. She's trying to avoid my eyes.

"Hey, nothin' to be embarrassed about. I love that I can do that to you. I'm gonna love it more when I'm inside you and you make those noises that set me off."

"Um, you didn't..." she stops, then tries again with,

"What about you...?" and stops again. I can see where she is going with this.

"Soon. Very soon. I am trying not to rush you Maddie." I can feel the strain in my cock and all I want to do is toss her onto her back and dive into her pussy until neither of us can breathe. But I can wait.

Maddie pulls herself up so she's level with me. "War, I'm not that innocent. I'm twenty-nine and I'm not a virgin." She lowers her head onto my chest. I feel her hand under her cheek, just over my heart.

"I get that. Now hear me: I want you to feel comfortable with me. I want us to be natural and relaxed when we get together. If you think you're ready, then we can talk about it tomorrow. It's been a long couple of days and I think we both need to get some sleep." I stroke her hair and continued, "Very soon, Baby. I'm not sure I am going to be able to wait much longer. Sleep for now."

I can feel her breath even out and I shut my eyes and drift into a blissful sleep holding my satisfied purring Kitten.

CHAPTER 10

Maddie's Story

War

I slowly shake away the remnants of sleep. Something feels off. I glance across to where my arm is already stretched across the bed towards a cool empty space. This pulls me straight out of my haze as I jerk out of bed and grab a worn pair of jeans, dragging them on hastily. I stalk toward the main rooms when I hear a faint humming. I continue towards the sound that now sounds more like soft singing, getting clearer as I approach the kitchen.

Maddie is wearing a tiny pair of shorts and an over-sized pink t-shirt with musical notes on it. It's so big on her that it drapes off one shoulder, baring her soft sexy skin. The same skin I tasted, licked and nipped at last night. I can still see the redness my scruff left on her nape. Her hair is up in a messy bun with tendrils hanging down around her face that she pushes back behind her ear as she stirs something in a bowl. Her little pink tongue and lips are making an incredible sound as she sways back and forth. She tips the bowl and allows batter to drizzle onto a griddle in front of her. She stops singing and I watch as her tongue sneaks out ever so slightly in concentration in making what I assume are pancakes. Her face lifts with a small smile and extends from ear to ear when she notices me staring at her. I'm leaning across the doorframe, arms crossed. Maddie makes the first move, diverting her eyes to grab the spatula and proceeds to flip the pancakes gently, making sure not to compromise their perfectly round shape.

I prowl towards her; moving to stand behind her and placing my hands on her hips to hold her steady. I placed my mouth right below the shell of her ear. I discovered this sensitive spot as I was exploring Maddie's body last night. A light breath expels from her lips and she closes her eyes; it's like she is trying to make a perfect memory. I love how her eyes flutter open again as if she's emerging from a deep satisfying dream. I continue to bestow a light flutter of kisses across her shoulder and neck.

She tilts her head up and back to meet my eyes. "Good morning, Honey."

The sweetest words I've ever heard from an angel I never dreamed would cross into my life. Soft and shy she raises herself to her tip toes and kisses my chin.

"Morning, Kitten." I growl in her ear. "You've been busy this morning."

"I thought I would surprise you with breakfast." She turns back to the pancakes and begins moving them from the griddle to the platter lying next to it. I pull back reluctantly to give her some space to move. It's then that I notice not only did she make me pancakes but set the table with fresh wild flowers too. She must have gone out exploring on her own this morning. I am going to have to talk to her about that but, not now. I don't want to risk that look of bliss on her face.

Maddie takes the coffee pot over to the table and begins pouring. "Aren't you hungry?" she asked as she continues to pour. I simply nod, entranced by her comfort in my kitchen. "Come on then. It's going to get cold and I want you try my secret recipe."

"Secret recipe?" I grin and raise my brows. "I bet I can get you to tell me the secret."

She smiles back brightly, the minx batting her eyes as she dares me. "Bet you can't. And I don't like cold pancakes. And if you want the chance to taste one while it's hot, I suggest you sit and eat with me."

I pull out my chair and sit, dragging my girl to my lap.

Maddie is unprepared for the sudden movement and flops down with a yelp of surprise. "War, what are you doing?"

I pull her plate and cutlery over to rest beside mine. "Stay here with me. I want you close." I move my hand up her back and feel her snuggle closer.

With that, she lifts her plate and cuts into her stack, spearing some pancake drizzling with golden syrup with her fork before raising it to my mouth. They could be cardboard and completely tasteless, and I will still think they're the most delicious flapjacks I've ever tasted. Lucky for me, they are extraordinary.

I moan my approval and she starts to giggle, forking more from her plate to take a bite herself.

By far, this is the best morning I have had since I was a kid at home with my mom. Mom worked long hours, but she made sure she always made Sunday morning special with breakfast together. When dad was killed in a car accident and she was left to raise a twelve-year-old boy on her own. I didn't realize how much of an effort it was for her to keep going after he died. She cried for months after the funeral, but then one day she just stopped. I was too young to see that mom was just going through the motions of living. I often feel a connection to Ava because she lost her parents young as well. Ava may be married to Guard but ever since she shared her story with me, I knew that we would always have that understanding of loneliness.

I was a good kid, but no matter what I did, Mom kept drifting deeper and deeper into a somber and sad place. Then one day that started like any other day, I came home to find her passed out on the sofa. I shook and shook her but couldn't get a response. I called the neighbors and they quickly called for an ambulance.

Suddenly, I was fifteen and alone by Mom's grave. Right next to Dad, because that's where she belonged. I was sent to foster care where I was transported from family to family, one bad situation to another. Until I finally turned eighteen and was turned out into the world with nothing and no one.

I quickly learned to fend for myself. I took whatever jobs was I could find and made sure I fed and clothed myself. I was attacked often because I wasn't a big kid. I was beaten up on the street and hustled more times than I cared to remember.

I was looking for shelter for the night when I was dragged into an alley by a gang of guys a little older than me. I thought I was going to die that night. I had no money to give them and they were so high they didn't care what they did to me. I screamed in pain when I was kicked in the back for what felt the hundredth time.

That's when I caught a blur of four men. They were huge, tattooed and fearless. They tore through my attackers; I could hear bones crunching, agonizing screams of pain, and then the thumps of bodies hitting the ground. My eyes were nearly swollen shut from the beating I had taken moments earlier and my body pulled into a ball to stop the pain in my ribs.

"We'll take him with us," I heard one of them say.

"He's not one of us," said another.

"None of us had each other until one of us decided we were worth it. I say he's worth it." He had a rough voice and that voice stays with me whenever I think of my brothers and what they did for me that night. Guard saved my life and my brothers took me in and made me part of their family. They picked me up and make sure I was nursed back to health. They taught me how to protect myself and in return I gave back all I had.

Guard let me prospect for two years and made sure I understood what total loyalty to the club meant. He saw that I had a talent for design and gave me a job in the shop customizing designs for the bikes and cars.

They called me War. Partly because I have raged a battle within myself, fighting to let go of the anger over the loss of my parents and partly because I'm a warrior for the MC. My intense desire to protect my brothers, has made me relentless in waging war against anyone who makes moves against us.

It's a gentle hand on my cheek that brings me back to the here and now. Maddie gazes at me with sad eyes and strokes my face with her soft gentle touch.

"You stopped eating. Is everything ok?" she asks tentatively.

"Everything is just as should be," I replied. I focussed on the beautiful girl in my arms, the warm delicious meal, and this feeling of happiness that has eluded me since I was a kid. In this singular moment, all is just right.

After finishing our meal, I tell Maddie to go get changed for company. I know it won't be long before the Vi and Ava team pounce. They seem determined to make every old lady is part of their inner circle. If I'm right, we have forty-five minutes tops before I hear the door chime.

I walk into the bedroom where I'm serenaded by the voice of my angel singing, "Hero." I move closer to the ensuite where I can hear her more clearly. When she sings, I can feel every word, every beat, every emotion.

I know I shouldn't, but I watch as she gently lathers her body, rinsing and moving her hands over her breasts and hips. I want my hands on her and I don't think I can hold off much longer before I take her and make her mine completely.

I strip down and step into the shower behind her. A startled roar of terror and wide eyes; Maddie is gasping for air. "Baby, it's me," I say quietly and pull her close, reaching behind her to shut off the water. "Hey, look at me. It's me," then again, "Look at me, Maddie." I tilt her chin upward so our eyes meet; I'm gutted by what see. Tears streaming down her cheeks, her body shuddering in fear; she is clearly pale and shaken.

"Christ, Baby, I didn't mean to scare you. I just wanted to be close to you." I continued to hold her as the tears subside, and her body relaxes. I turn the water back on to rinse us both, then after draping a towel around myself, I wrapped her in a towel and set her on the center of the bed. I climb behind her and wrap myself around her like a cloak. I want her to feel my warmth and strength. "You're safe, Kitten. I will never let anyone hurt you. Ever!" I say with steely determination.

Maddie takes a deep breath, turning her head to the side and upward so that we are staring into one another's eyes.

"I'm so sorry. I never wanted you to have to see me this way," She takes another breath and continues while fidgeting with the hem of the towel enveloping her body. "It must be the new place, new routine, and new everything. I feel like an idiot." She stops suddenly and diverts her eyes from mine, making a move to distance herself from me.

"None of that," I say sternly and place my forehead against hers. "There is no reason to apologise. I knew your history and make a stupid decision. I'm the one who's sorry. I never want you to feel unsafe." I kissed her softly. Small butterfly kisses until I can feel the anxiety ease out of her body. "Kitten, I never want you to hide what you're feeling or thinking. Promise me."

"I promise," she mumbles as her arms round the back of my neck, bringing her face close. "I wasn't always like this, War. I was a normal person." I hear her hiccup and know that a flow of tears is about to bubble to the surface again.

"Baby, when you're ready, I am here to listen to what happened. All of it. I want to know so we can work through this together. I want to know who he was; how long he had you; what he said. I want to know it all, and once you let it all out, we can heal. And I will tell you my story, so you can understand why my brotherhood and the "Pride" mean so much to me."

"Not now," she replies faintly. "Soon, I promise." Her grip doesn't lessen but I'm comforted in the fact that her breathing regulates.

I continue to kiss her softly, all over her beautiful face. Little kisses on her eyes, cheeks and lips. I can feel her shift and wriggle to connect her body closer to mine. She is getting totally turned on. I place her astride me with her knees on other side of my hips as I lean back into to the headboard. Her fingers trace the tattoos on my arms, then veer their path to my chest making an exploratory journey through her gentle touch. I feel her lips on the edge of the tattooed Celtic cross; I had it etched onto my skin as way to pay tribute to my family, with births and deaths inscribed within it.

Her body melds further into mine, I can feel her core pressing hard against my cock. I am already holding on by a thread and my Maddie isn't make this any easier. I wrap her hair around my fist and tug to slam her mouth against mine. Her lips soften, open and give it all back to me.

"Please," she begs as she grinds down on me.

"Fuck, Baby, are you sure?" I ask hoarsely. I barely recognize my own vice. I am silently begging that she doesn't want to stop. Little moans escape her lips and she nods her head, growling *yes* into my ear. I flip her onto her back and move my hands to slide under her towel. I continue to savour the look in her eyes as I remove the towel completely. My mouth makes its way from her throat, licking, sucking and tasting the path that leads down to her erect nipples, teasing me with their sweet rose colouring. A soft moan leaves those perfect lips as I tug on one rosy tip ever so gently. The more I lap and suck her pert nipple, the louder her moans become, her hands now griping my hair, holding me to her breasts. She curves her back forcing her breast further into my mouth. She tastes incredible.

A cold splash of water hits when I her the loud buzz from the front door. A few seconds later and the buzz is continuous. I can hear Maddie panting in my ear, but I know that whoever that is will not be deterred. Those two women are not going to leave.

The buzzing has turned to pounding and I carefully move away from Maddie. I speak with a low shallow breath, trying to get myself in control. "Baby, someone is here and they're not going to leave," I relay the news, my cock is protesting with throbbing need.

She looks completely bemused. "Okay," she says quietly. I pull myself away with a groan. I look closer and notice uncertainty and quickly move to reassure her. "They're friends, baby. Annoying, intrusive friends but true friends," I tease.

"Get dressed, Baby. Come down when you're ready. I have to go answer that door before they break and enter," I joke but also know they would do it.

I tag my jeans and throw them on, then grab Maddie once more and kiss her soundly on the mouth. "Hurry, Baby. I'm not sure how long I can hold them off,"

She smiles back, and it lights up my soul; tilting her head slightly and biting her lower lip before she nods shyly.

I head to open the door for the two women I admire most in the Satan's Pride crew. They are standing with hands on hips waiting impatiently for me to let them in. I barely get the door open when I'm shoved to the side by a very pregnant Ava. Actually, I let her push me out of the way. Our little Ava thinks she is fierce and none of the Satan's Pride have the heart to tell her that although her heart is fierce, she is still a tiny thing, even when pregnant.

Vi, on the other hand, has always been generous and accommodating. She has been dating our second in command for a couple of years. As a matter of fact, Vi was the first woman that was taken seriously in our crew. Orion and she started their relationship within the first few months of us settling in this town. Orion has never labelled their relationship to "old lady" status and may never have declared Vi formally as such, but no one in the crew would treat her with anything less than full respect. Lately, Vi has been quieter than her usual boisterous self. Her smile lacks luster. I have a weird feeling about it. This is Orion's business and unless asked, I keep out of it. Today is my lucky day because Vi's smile is lit up like a beacon, mainly due to Ava's nuttiness. The girls are looking for my girl and make no pretense about it.

"Hi, War, is Maddie here?" Ava asks while making her way into my kitchen.

"Not in there, doll," I counter, laughing at the inspection of my home.

"You didn't scare her off, already did you? Cause if you did, I'm going to unleash the Kraken on you. I like Maddie and Vi and I are looking forward to forming a kick ass "lady pride" group." Ava gives me a withering stare with her hand on a hip and a massive protruding belly.

I can't help it, I laugh so hard I think I'm going to piss myself. I laugh to the point where Vi starts giggling because I can't stop. Unfortunately, I forget to consider the highly emotional state Ava has been in lately and a flood of tears start. Vi runs over to console Ava and I reign myself in.

"What the hell, Ava?" a gruff deep voice bellows from across the room. This is a fine time for Guard to show up with a prospect in tow. Cris has been on watch for the last few days and Guard is giving him some higher duties to test his reliance and loyalty.

"War made me cry!" she says as her tears are mopped up by a very attentive Vi.

Guard diverts his attention my way and I shrug. "No way. I am not to blame. Anyone—and I mean anyone—would have laughed their asses off over this scene. I'm sure Maddie would love some girl time with you two so grab a seat."

Maddie comes into the sitting area to see Guard in my armchair with Ava on his lap. Vi is standing next to the fireplace, leaning and watching Guard talk softly to his wife. Vi's eyes are soft as she observes how easily Guard turns Ava's tears into a magnanimous smile.

As soon as I see my girl, I cross the room and tag her hand. "Hey, Kitten, look who came by to visit us today." I stand behind her, my arms curled around her middle.

"Hey," she says, smiling at the scene. "What's going on guys? I heard you laughing," she says as she turns her head up to me. "What's so funny?"

"I'll explain later, Baby," I whisper in her hair.

Maddie turns to Vi. "Hi, I'm Maddie."

"Hey, Maddie, I'm Vi. I'm Orion's gal. I saw you perform the other night. You are amazing. I love your music. You are so incredibly talented." She walks over to us and tugs Maddie out of my arms and hugs her tight. "It's great to have you here," she says firmly.

Ava runs to congregate with the other girls. "Me too!" she cries out and settles herself into a group hug with my woman and Vi. Maddie's smile is beaming, and I love Vi and Ava even more than I did fifteen minutes ago, for allowing Maddie into their fold.

"So, no guys, please," Ava remarks. "We want to have girl time."

"Ava, this is my house," I remind her teasingly.

She looks over to Guard, "Don't you have any place you can send him?" she asks cheekily, as she points directly at me.

"Ava!" Guard says sternly "This is War's home, but if I know my brother, he will gladly walk away so you ladies can start talking about whatever it is you talk about. No matter what, Cris stays with you until we get back. He'll be outside the door." I can tell that he says this for Maddie's benefit. He is aware of her fearful nature and wants to reassure that she is always with the Pride. He turns to me, "Come on, man. I have some shit to discuss with you. Let's take a ride."

"Yeah, right behind you," I say. I make my way to my girl and kiss her hard on the mouth, then rumble in her ear, "Be good. And remember where we were for later." I wink at her and follow Guard out the door.

Twenty minutes later and we are sitting at the club meeting table with Orion, Risk, and Demon. When the guys follow Guard and I into the room, I knew this was not going to be a simple disclosure of information regarding to Maddie's kidnapping. Orion is a master at uncovering information and I told him to dig and dig deep.

"Well, how is the old man?" Orion smirks and lifts an eyebrow.

"Not funny, man. You tell me—you've been hooked up longer than I have," I reply.

Orion's lips go firm and tense. I'm about to ask what gives when Guard stands up and says, "Look, let's get this shit out, so we can set up some safety measures." Guard turns to me and continues, "Orion has been digging around and came up with some information about Maddie's abduction." He looks at Orion nods to imply he should take over the discussion.

"His name is Jefferson Hendley. He is 32 years old. After he abducted Maddie he was sentenced to a psychiatric facility. Two and a half months ago, he was released into the custody of his parents, who live a two-and-a-half-hour drive from her apartment. As part of his recovery and release, he must attend weekly counselling sessions with a psychiatrist. He has made it to every one so far." He pauses, then starts again with, "Here's the fucked-up shit that happened before he took Maddie. A year prior, he started writing her letters. No one took much notice because the band getting fan mail all the time. The content seemed harmless enough, typical shit. He loves her, wants her, dreams about how good they are together. He got no response, so the notes started turning aggressive. He got crude; calling her a slut and a tease. Says she throws herself at the men in the audience. Then he starts sounding cracked and goes on about how she needs to be disciplined and how he's going to make sure that once they were together, she would never stray." Orion takes a breath. "That last bit is a direct quote from the last letter he sent her."

"What the fuck!" I can't control my anger. I'm gripping the end of the table with white knuckles. I have to let go of the anger before I lose my shit. I slam my fist into the table, knocking everything clear onto the floor with a horrible crash. I move to get up and Guard says, "Hey, sit down. You need to hear it all. I hate to feed you this shit, but you need to know it, so we can be prepared."

"What else?" I look at Orion. He blows out a long breath.

"That night he went to the concert. He had been to so many of them that the security men knew him. He never let on that he had any anger issues and showed no outward signs of aggressiveness; so, when they were giving out back stage passes, they let him have one."

He paused for a minute and looked at Guard; he nodded for Orion to keep going. "This is where it gets really whacked. You need to keep your shit together." He looked down at the table and went on. "Maddie was with the rest of the band. They were drinking and having a good time. Maddie was still young, so her brother made sure to keep an eye on her. They found out later that someone drugged his drink. He crashed on the sofa and when he came to, he saw the rest of the group passed out and Maddie was missing."

"Jesus!" I yell out and draw a hand down across my face and across to the back of my neck. "And?" I push Orion for more.

"When the police were called, they found signs of a struggle and small amounts of blood. The security team saw Maddie leave with Jeff and saw that she was acting weird but were busy controlling the crowds." Orion started walking around the table. "This is where everything gets fuzzy. He had her for twenty-four hours. Never asked for ransom. They traced him with the information security gave. When they found them, Maddie had a cut on her face and bruises on her arms and legs. Her clothes were torn, and she was huddled in a corner of the room she was being held. He held her at knife point and threatened to kill her if they tried to take her from him. The police report states they were able to disarm him when he became distracted by Maddie sobbing and started trying to console her. When he went to pull her close the officer saw an opportunity and took that second to pounce and take him down."

I look around the table at my brothers. I knew this tell-all isn't over yet. "Go on, I know there's something you aren't telling me." The silence is killing me. "Do I have to beat it out of you?" I stand and walk to Orion, look him right in the eye. "Let me have it. I need to know," I say through clenched teeth.

"Maddie has said little to nothing about the whole incident. She was admitted to hospital but wouldn't let the doctors or nurses touch her. Her brother was the only one she let hold her or even come near her. They finally had to sedate her to treat her for her injuries. She had a black eye, 2 cracked ribs, cuts and bruises and a sprained ankle. They wanted to test for rape but needed her permission. She refused. She got so upset when they tried to approach her that she ripped her IV out of her arm and tried to run." Orion stops, places his hand on my shoulder and glares into my eyes, his expression pained. "There's nothing on the record, but chances are, she may have been raped."

I moved for the door when Guard pulls me back. "Hold up brother. I need you to calm the fuck down before you let your woman see you like this."

I shake him off. Demon stands and bars the entrance. I turn to face my Pride family.

"Take a deep breath, man," Risk says. "We are here to do whatever you need but whatever we do, we do it right. So be cool and let's hear it all."

"Hear it all?" I repeat. "You tell me there's more? What the fuck more can there be? My woman is at home, without me. She has been through hell and hasn't said a fucking word to anyone. That shit is going to eat at her gut until there's a gaping wound so raw that it eats her alive." At this point I am fucking screaming at the top of my lungs in the face of my most trusted friends.

Risk pulls me down into a chair next to him. "This is the last bit, and after this, we can decide on a course of action."

I place my head in my hands, "Fuck, okay, say it," I growl.

"Jeff has been spotted in and around Maddie's old apartment by some shopkeepers," Risk says. "I know because I spoke with them. We need to be careful about how to we move on this. We don't want Maddie hearing and freaking out even more. So far, this guy hasn't done anything the police can arrest him on. A restraining order only works if he is caught and is only a deterrent at this point."

Guard stands tall. "Maddie is one of us. She is your old lady and our family now. We protect our family."

I look at my family, one at a time. I see the determination on their faces. I see loyalty.

"I need to get home to Maddie. I don't want to be away from her, especially now," I grind out.

"Listen, War, I think we are jumping the gun. We haven't got proof he is sniffing around for her yet. We need to be diligent and smart." Risk is always so rational and systematic, even though he's risked his own life repeatedly to protect his buddies. His sniper training from back when he was enlisted has left him so precise and clear in thought, making him methodical and relentless. He is dangerous as fuck and I, for one, am glad he's on our side.

"Here's the plan, men," Guard pipes up. "Risk, you're in charge of setting up proper security at War's place. Orion keep digging. I want to know where this guy lives and where he is right now! Demon you work a schedule where Maddie always has a man on her and I do mean always. When War is working the club, someone is assigned to Maddie. And seeing that the women have now formed bonds, we need to make sure that Ava and Vi are covered too."

Orion responds first. "Deep breath, man. We aren't going to let that little pissant get away with shit."

Risk moves closer to me and by his twisted lips and far-away look, I can tell his mind is whirling into motion.

"Say it!" I demand.

"Hear me out: We should tell Vi and Ava about the basics of what we are looking out for." We all start to shake our heads to say no way and he holds his hands out to stop us. "If they are aware that there's maybe a threat, they can be smart about where they go together and make it easier to keep them all safe."

"Not yet," Guard announces. "Let's give this a few weeks to see where we're at before we decide."

I walk out letting my brothers know by the chin lifts and handshakes that they are appreciated. I'm on my way back to my girl. I am so wretched with anger, if I had that fucker in my grasp, he wouldn't be alive long. I have never backed down from a fight. I have stood behind my brothers, I have led them as well. When we've been threatened, I have made those who threaten us pay. I have been pissed before, but nothing like I feel right now. I could rip Jeff's heart from his chest and feel no remorse.

I feel anguished over the thought of my Maddie terrified for a full twenty-four hours, being held and abused. I knew she was shaken by what happened, but until today, I had no idea the extent of the damage she endured at the hands of that freak.

As I ride my chopper home, I'm able to calm down somewhat. The last thing I want is to give her an inkling that anything is off.

I'm just outside the room when I hear the girls giggling. Quietly, I glimpse in and see my Maddie put her hands to her belly, holding it while leaning back on the sofa with tears streaming down her cheeks.

"Okay, okay, seriously, I want to know how serious it's gotten with War," Ava asks.

"Um, I guess we are just getting to know one another," Maddie replies.

"Come on. Spill," Vi leans into her and hugs her close. "We just want to make sure you are good with everything. I know that this all happened really fast for you."

"I'm good. War is sweet. He is being very careful with me," Maddie answers, then drops her eyes to her lap. "Can I ask you guys something about War?"

"Sure. Not sure how much help we'll be. He is a pretty private guy. I can tell you he is loyal and dedicated to the Satan's Pride," Vi replies.

"Does he have a lot of girlfriends?" Maddie asks.

Vi and Ava look at one another. Ava is the first to speak, "He has had his fair share of woman, Maddie. He's not a saint and I can honestly say that since he met you, and I mean met you at the studio, I have not seen him with anyone else."

"Oh, okay." Maddie shifts in her seat. "I am not sure he really wants me. He kisses me and stuff, but he hasn't..." Her voice falters and she goes silent.

Vi takes her hand, "Listen here, he does want you. I know that look when a guy wants his woman. He is probably giving you some time to get used to all the changes." She smiles and continues. "I think that's really sweet of him."

Maddie looks at them both then rushes through her next words. "I don't want him to stop and he keeps stopping." The look of pure confusion on her face says it all. "Maybe I'm doing it wrong." It comes out as more of a question than a statement.

I listen to the words coming out of her mouth and am shocked that she would think I don't want her. Here I am trying to move slow to not spook her. Well, this changes everything. I was worried I was moving too fast for her.

"Honey, you are doing nothing wrong. You can try making it a special night with you making the first move. I know it can be a little intimidating, but you can put on something special, light some candles, and maybe play him one of your songs. The man loves how you sing," Ava says.

"I don't know if I can do sexy," Maddie says as she bites her lower lip.

I've heard enough. I enter the room, making enough noise to make the ladies aware that I am back. "Hey lovelies." I walk over to my girl and kiss her soundly on the mouth. No mistaking from that kiss that I want her. "Hello, Kitten, have you been behaving yourself?" I tease her and squeeze her close to me.

Ava struggles to get off the sofa, "Of course we have been. What could happen here with our guard dog stationed outside?" She makes a fist and points her thumb to the door leading out to the terrace where I notice Cris standing at attention.

"Is Orion coming to pick me up?" Vi asks. She has definitely not been herself lately. There is hesitancy in her words. She's normally so vivacious.

"No, Cris is going to drop you off," I say. I motion to Cris and wait for him to get close enough before I say, "Take Ava and Vi home. You do a walk through before you leave them if the guys aren't there. You understand?"

I make sure we have eye contact and he sees the seriousness of my expression without raising my tone. I don't want our ladies freaking about anything until Guard is ready. He is our leader and I trust him.

"Got it." Cris nods his head and I can tell he understands the severity of the situation. He has come a long way as a prospect and has served us well. When things calm down, I plan to call for a vote to get him fully patched in. He has given us everything and has always put the club first.

"Hey, War, just want to let you know that we have packed up the other boxes you asked for and are delivering them here tomorrow morning. I also made arrangements for Rod to come out here to give you an estimate on the recording studio," Cris says.

"Thanks, Cris. I appreciate you taking the lead on that," I tell him proudly.

"I've left two sets of plans on the kitchen table. Have a look. Risk put them together and says he'll do the finishing work but prefers that Rod does the structure." Cris walks to the front door, then addresses the ladies. "Ava, Vi, I'll bring the car closer. I don't want you tripping, Ava. Guard would have my head." He saunters out the door. Ava giggles and Vi rolls her eyes.

"That man is awesome. If I didn't love Orion so much, I would have a go at him," Vi adds.

I hear the sound of an angel laughing as I look at Maddie, whose pink lips are wide with giggles. I have never witnessed a more heavenly site. I gather her closer in my arms and kiss her nose. "You're beautiful," I state simply.

CHAPTER 11

Take the Lead, Maddie

Maddie

The rest of our day consisted of quiet time. We threw on some movies and lounged about on the couch. It didn't go unnoticed that I hummed along to every theme song that played. War says it's cute; I bobbed my head and tapped my fingers in time with the beat. I'm happy; I feel like my old self. The only other time I have ever been this content was when I was singing or when I slept in War's arms. Those were also the times when I felt most beautiful.

As the last movie come to an end, War asks, "What do you feel like for dinner?" A casual arm is draped across my shoulders. I twist to look up at him. I love those eyes and those soft lips. I can't help myself and lean in to kiss him; I want to feel his lips on mine. I take my time, exploring how soft yet firm his lip feels and taste. I want him to take over and take us both to ecstasy. How do I let him know I'm ready to take to bed and fully explore one another? It feels so right. I can't help myself and moan with need.

War pulls back before I can do anything to stop him. "Dinner?" he asks in his gruff voice, our brows colliding.

"I can cook. I make a great pasta. Do you like pasta?" I ask, excited.

"Love it. Let's make sure we have all the ingredients you need, or we are going to have to make a grocery run."

After I start dinner, I decide that Ava and Vi are right. I need to make a firm statement to let War know that I am ready for him. I pop into the bedroom and head straight for the closet, pulling out the few dresses I have. I rarely go out anywhere, so I have a limited variety to choose from apart from my stage clothes and those are over the top. I save those for the concerts.

A year ago, I had decided to spend a little more energy on how I looked. I had become so consumed with hiding that I realized I did it with my clothes too. I created a barrier with over-sized clothing in very basic colours that allowed me to blend into the background. I felt so dirty after the kidnapping that I stayed in sweats. I had to take my life back; this started with the simple act of choosing a dress that I would be willing to wear. It seemed like a small thing to do but for me it was a huge battle I won when I was able to choose the dress I was now holding so lovingly in my hands. Yes, it was pretty. But it meant much more, I took a piece of myself back that day.

I put it on and look at the reflection in the mirror; I see me. The Maddie I am now and the Maddie with plans to become even more great. The dress is a strapless form-fitted piece that falls to just above my knees in a sky blue. It's a simple cut that fits like a glove and enhances my silhouette. I have curves and this dress certainly shows them. I decide to put on makeup, just enough to accent my cheeks and eyes with soft colours and highlight my lips in a blush pink.

I hear the timer and jet back into the kitchen to wrap up the final touches on our meal. I look at the dinner table, feeling a little nervous. I forge ahead!

"War, dinner is ready," I call out to him. He's in his office working through paperwork, which he hates. I'd help him, but truth be told, I'd suck at it too.

War saunters to the table and stops abruptly. His eyes peruse the tablecloth, candles, and napkins. Then his gaze heads in my direction and he sizes me up from head to toe. Taking in my killer 4-inch heels, his eyes move thoroughly back up again to my face, hair, and at last his eyes meet mine. I stare back, and it is safe to say he does it better and sexier. There is a heat in his eyes; heat I saw before, when we were in bed this morning. I think he is ready to pounce. War takes a few steps toward me and walks around my chair, motioning for me to sit. He lowers his lips to my ear and whispers in that raw, gravelly voice, "I know what I am having for dessert."

My cheeks are flushed, and my eyes are soft, and I think I want dessert too.

Dinner with War is easy. Our conversations flow and he talks about the studio plans he was reviewing and wants me to take a look at them tomorrow to make sure that nothing I want or need is missing. He asks about my brother and family. I tell him more about my parents and our semi-relationship. We chat about our likes and dislikes. I learned that he hates eggplant and I vow to make him change his mind. I love eggplant. I want him to try my eggplant parmesan. I swear he will love it after that. He teases me about the suitcases I packed, claiming there were more books than clothes. He's almost right. It is light and fun.

We are both done dinner and I innocently asked if he would like to try my dessert. I immediately remembered what he'd whispered to me before dinner and feel the heat rising to my cheeks. I stammer out, " I made a homemade key lime pie."

His laugh fills the air, his head falls back, and his eyes light up with sheer happiness. I can't help but laugh too. "Come here, Kitten," he calls and extends a hand my way.

I rise from my chair on shaky legs, take his hand to find my way on his lap, my knees between his legs, my arm around his shoulders and I am still smiling from his laughter.

"I think we should save dessert for later, Baby," he mumbles. His fingers slid up my back and up into my hair and he lowers my mouth to meet his.

That smoldering gaze returns. His tongue traces my lips and then becomes bolder as he gently nips and tastes them. Slow, sensuous, long, and torturously feverish. The electricity is piercing every part of my body. I mold my arms around his nape and press closer to his chest. The hand on my knee trails upward, sliding upward to my outer thigh. Up, up until it slides under the hem of my dress caressing me softly. War's fingers are rough, the hands of a mechanic, yet his touch is soft, and the roughness feels erotic against my skin. His hand moves across my leg to my inner thighs, gently widening my legs. I willingly part my thighs and wait in anticipation for his touch. He lifts his mouth from mine, "Baby, look at me," he commands. "See me," he directs. I open my eyes and feel his lips touch mine and his fingers slide under my black lace thong, inching towards my centre.

A moan escapes and I whisper a breathless, "Yes," against his lips, not wanting to lose contact with them.

His finger begins to slide through my folds, around and around my clit until I'm desperate for more of his touch. I move my body further into his hand, pressing down to alleviate my intense need for relief. A simple movement and his finger slides inside me, feeling the sticky wetness before it slides back out to swirl over my clit again and again.

The pressure draws me nearer and nearer to what I know will be a fevered orgasm. I squirm greedily in his lap. I feel his hard cock straining against his jeans. "Please, War, please," I say in a desperate whisper. His finger fucks me in a steady rhythm. I want him so badly, I reach down and grasp his cock over his jeans letting him know that I'm ready for more.

With the same rhythm as his hand I press against his cock. "Honey, please I need madre. I want you. I want this," I say, my body trembling with desire and my voice is so sultry that I barely recognize it.

War stands, taking me with him, stalking with steely determination to our bedroom. He sets me on my feet taking care that I am firmly planted. Without pause he drops his mouth to mine, kissing me deeper and longer with excruciating intensity. Then with quiet calmness he commands, "Turn around, Kitten."

I turn to face the bed and fingers at the zipper of my dress slowly slide down. His lips touch each inch of exposed skin. So slow, painfully slow. I wait for each touch of his lips. At last, the zipper ends just above my rounded ass and I feel his lips linger there and then trace the same path upward all over again with his lips, keeping my hips steady. For this I am grateful because I'm on shaky legs. My heart beats harder and faster. I want to touch him, but he holds me firm in his hands. The dress is lowered to my waist and delicate flutter kisses braze over my shoulders and into the nape of my neck. My dress drops to the floor leaving me in my scant lace thong. War's hands roam over my ass cheeks and smooth over my skin delicately like he is taking in every inch of my body. His hand wraps around my waist and glides up to cup my breasts with his lips still working at the hot spot between my neck and shoulder. His hands squeeze my breasts lightly as his teeth nip at the pleasure spot at my shoulder. I gasp and shiver at his touch. I lean back against his hard muscled and toned body.

My hands cover his at my breasts and suddenly I am aware that I am almost naked, and he is still fully dressed. I press back and rub my ass against his cock.

"On the bed, Maddie," his voice is filled with lust and need. I walk two steps forward to the bed and crawled my way onto it, giving War a full view of my ass jiggling as I move. I look over my shoulder to see

War toss his t-shirt across the room before he kicks off his boots then walks with narrow focus to the bed. I admire his perfect physique. He is a statue of perfection, the scars on his skin make him even more sexy.

"Undo my belt, Maddie," he commands. His hands firmly grip my hair as I kneel at the edge of the bed. My hands move to his belt and release catch, followed by the button and zipper. I want to keep going but War lays me back against the pillows as he tugs his jeans and boxers off.

He is magnificent. My warrior. His knees now sit between my splayed legs, the lightest touch of his fingertips explore my ankles, legs, then slowly ascend higher and higher. My breath hitches and I become more fevered and impatient. I am rewarded for my supreme patience when his body looms over mine, our bodies grazing one another, and his lips find mine. Deep and wet. A kiss penetrating with hunger filling your body's every need and yet leaves you desperate for the next taste and touch. The more we kiss the more my body craves his. My hands move to explore his body curving around to his back pulling him closer to remove the space between us, wanting to fuse our bodies together.

He takes my hands in his and places them by either side of my head, fingers lace together as he laves my breasts with wet kisses and licks at my nipples. His tongue licks and flicks my nipples until they are hard and achy, then takes them fully into his mouth, suckling on one then the other. I feel the wetness pool between my legs. More. I need more and lift my hips communicating without words the sheer need to connect our bodies together.

"Shh, Baby, let's savour this. Nice and slow, Kitten. I want you with everything that I am, but I am going to take my time with you. With us." War groans as he lifts his head from my breast; wet kisses blaze a trail lower and lower, heating my body that is already prepared to combust. He stops at my core.

My wide-spread legs are being held apart by his shoulders. I am open and vulnerable, but also thrilled and excited for more of him. Teasing me, his lips slide lower and lower until he is right there and his tongue flicks at my nub. My fingers clench intertwined in his as his mouth closes fully over my nub, sucking and licking until all sense escapes me and I am begging for release.

I can hardly recognize my own moans and pants growing louder and more frenzied. I cry out in frustration, straining for that ultimate release. At that moment, War latches onto my clit and suckles so intently it elicits a cataclysmic orgasm.

With hazy eyes and gasping breath, I find my focus on the most beautiful face watching my every movement with soft hushes and murmuring words of telling me how incredible I look when I come.

"I'm not finished, Baby. I want more; I want it all. I need to be inside you." His voice is strained.

He turns me onto my stomach and begins another assault on my senses. Positioning me on my hands and knees, running his hands over my ass, up and over the small of my back and around to tease my nipples. Tugging gently and rolling the tips between his thumbs and forefingers. My body reacts and presses further into his caress.

A hand moves down and over my belly to the lips of my sex. I am so wet that he has no problem slipping his finger between my pussy lips and penetrates, easing his finger in and out. "Oh, yes," I breath out. "Don't stop." I am frantic and needy, trying to push myself over the edge again. I whimper and beg. "Please don't stop."

"I'll always give you what you need." His voice sounds anguished. His cock hard and thick, rubbing against my inner thigh.

"I need you inside me. Come inside me, Honey." We are both hot and hungry for each other. His mouth nips at the base of my neck and my pussy spasms with his fingers inside me, still teasing me to the brink of yet another orgasm. Oh my God, his lips move across my neck and shoulders and I move my lower body to erratically fuck myself on his fingers.

"I am going to take you slow, Baby," he says. Damn slow! I need him now, hard and fast. His cock is set at the entrance to my pussy and I push back to take all of him as soon as I feel the tip near my dripping sex. Steady hands at my waist hold me still as his wide thick cock penetrates me deeper and deeper. Inch after inch, I moan, slurring my words and begging him to let me come. I can hear his tortured and raspy groans as he fully settles inside me. He is huge, and I feel so full. We take a moment to fully embrace our union. "Maddie you feel so good. So tight. Made for me, Baby. You were made for me."

"Xander, please move, Honey. I need you to move." I wriggle my ass, letting him know that I am ready to take all that he can give me. He pulls out and then with a hard deep thrust he is inside me again. I gasp at the thrill. My body clenches at his cock each time he thrusts in and out. His movements become more aggressive and faster; that twinge of ecstasy returned with fervour. Each time our bodies slap together, I hear his groan becoming more audible.

When I think I can take no more, I feel Xander's body cloak protectively over mine. His hands find mine and intertwine our fingers. We are completely connected thighs to chest, skin on skin, his mouth by my ear hoarsely whispers, "Come for me, my Maddie. Let me hear you." As if on command, I come immediately. I was still riding the last of my euphoria when I hear the roar of his release and his pulsating cock in my pussy. So powerful and exhilarating.

We stay connected until our breathing returns to normal. Slowly Xander pulls out making sure not to hurt me, moving onto his back and turning me to lay beside him with my head resting on his chest. I feel the touch of his lips in my hair. Sweet and gentle, I have never felt more loved.

"That was the best seduction dinner ever, Baby. I am going to want and expect more of those," he says while pulling me up to kiss the tip of my nose.

"I was trying to be subtle," I giggle. He roared with laughter. I am happy to know that I can make him do that. "Do you want me to go get dessert and we can have key lime pie in bed?" I ask. "Honestly, it's really good. I make a great pie."

"I bet you do, Kitten. But I'll get the pie and you stay right where you are." War climbs out of bed fully uninhibited by his lack of clothing. He prowled out the bedroom door and is back with key lime pie in tow. The view is stupendous from both the back and the front.

I did notice that he forgot something though. "You forgot the plates and forks. I'll get them," I say, making the move to jump out of bed. War grips my hand to keep me in place.

I see a glint in his eye. "Nope. Don't need them. I am making a new dessert—Key Lime Maddie Pie." He takes his finger and dips it into the pie before smearing the mixture on my lips before devouring them.

The pie is delicious. I have Key Lime with a taste of War and he has his served with Maddie.

Best Pie Ever.

CHAPTER 12

Making Room

We lounged in bed all evening. I slept with Maddie pinning me to the bed with legs so soft and smooth I was tempted more than once to wake her by making love to her again. The early morning light shone brightly on my shy seductress. I am here with an angel in my arms.

I knew that she was going all out to make dinner special last night. I had no idea I was going to be entertained by a goddess in a dress that could melt any ice heart. The dress was impressive. I looked her up and down and down and up and I still couldn't get over the extraordinary beauty I'm lucky enough to be with. The amazing curves, soft pink lips, now swollen from out passionate kisses, and that hair spread across the pillows in soft curls; a very tempting site. I resist the urge to reach out and wake her. I force myself out of bed and into the shower. I let the stream of fresh cool water run over my body hoping it will tame my cock into behaving. I close my eyes and remember how desperately my Maddie begged me to take her. Almost as badly as I wanted her. It took every ounce of willpower to slow myself down and take her with care. I should be fully sated as I woke her twice last night to take her again, working her clit with my fingers until she woke and urged me to slide into her. The soft murmurs and hitches in her breath are addictive; I can't get enough of her. I fist my cock and work myself to relieve the pressure building. I let the memory of last night take the edge off and finish my shower.

I force myself to dress quickly and not look back to the bed where I know I will return if I see her sweet pout. Coffee. I need coffee.

The view was the reason I bought this property. I look out and see trees and hear the brook gurgling in the distance. It was peaceful and serene, and I want to come home knowing that this is waiting for me. I kick back in an Adirondack chair, lifting the cup to take my first sip of coffee, watching this view knowing that soon Maddie will be up to share all of this with me. Perfection. I haven't felt this right since I was a kid and mom and dad were with me.

My thoughts are interrupted by a dishevelled Maddie in my t-shirt reaching down to her upper thighs showing just a hint of pink lace panties. She too is holding a mug, taking her first dose of caffeine. "Mmmm," she sighs after the warm liquid slides down her throat. Everything she does turns me on. At this rate I am going to be spending a shit load of time taking cold showers.

"Here, Baby," I call to her. Without reservation, Maddie comes across the deck and makes herself comfortable, sharing my chair with her legs thrown over mine. Her hands wrap around her mug and she takes small sips, enjoying the view. No words needed, just two people taking in the serenity of the universe and each other. Perfection.

I have been tempered by experience and conditioned to use my senses. When I hear the rumbling of bikes nearing the house, I inform Maddie, "We have company."

"I better get changed and start breakfast."

I hold her still and she meets my eyes.

"First you say good morning, Kitten, then you go get dressed," I say, letting my hand feel the softness of her skin.

"Oh sorry!" she says popping her head up, her smile beaming, "Good morning, Honey." She tries once again to move, and I still hold tight. She looks confused.

"I want a proper good morning," I tease, "with tongue." With Maddie all I have to do is ask and she winds her arms around my neck, being careful not to spill our coffees as she proceeds to rock my world with the taste of her. I lift my hand to cup her breast and move my lip to her temple, giving her a sweet kiss. In return, she cups my jaw and lets her mouth move over mine, running her tongue across my lips, dipping in so that we are fused together. I reluctantly pull back knowing we are due for company any moment.

"Good morning, War," she sighs.

"Yeah, good morning War," I hear Risk's voice coming from the sliding door off the kitchen leading to the deck.

Maddie jumps up from my lap, letting out a squeak, "I'll just go get changed." She runs past Risk and through the door he just vacated. Then she pops her head back out, keeping the rest of her hidden behind the wall. "Morning Risk, will you be joining us for breakfast?"

"That would be great, Maddie. I haven't had time to grab anything yet," Risk replies. She smiled back at him.

I have an urge to rip his head off. My best friend, as far as I'm concerned, and I'm about ready to knock him out. I saw his grin and I push out of my chair. I punch him in the shoulder, probably harder than I should.

"What the hell?" he asks, rubbing his shoulder and shoving me back.

"Why are you here?" I ask, ignoring his question. I know I'm being an asshole, but I haven't had enough time alone with Maddie.

"Hey man, this is on you," he says, still grinning like a fool.

"How's that?" I ask confused.

"You said to get her stuff here and it will be here in a half hour. You wanted the security setup ASAP— your words—so that's happening too. And you wanted to start construction on the studio. I need to get those plans finalized today if you want to start work on that and finish on the timeline we discussed. So, don't shoot the messenger. I wanted to prep you for the onslaught of brothers showing up in less than an hour." He stands with his hands on his hips, smirking at me.

"Shit," I say but I know Risk is right. Maddie's comfort and safety are my main priority. "Sorry, man. I just thought I had a little more time this morning."

"I don't blame you for wanting time alone with your woman and it's because she is yours we want to make sure that we have taken every precaution." That's Risk, calm and matter-of-fact. "We are calling this a moving-in party cause I know you don't want to freak her out. Ava and Vi are coming by to help her unpack and keep her busy while we work out here, setting up the cameras and equipment."

"Thanks for setting this all up Risk. I do appreciate all the effort and time you put into this," I say genuinely. I don't want Maddie to catch on that I am concerned about her stalker out hunting, obsessed with my woman.

"Not me alone. We all decided, and Guard wants everyone on high alert until we locate this shithead," he informs me. Then his grin gets bigger and adds, "I think you should count on more company for breakfast and lunch. You know our brothers can eat."

I shake my head and see the humor in all this. "Christ, I better get the prospects to pick up more groceries." I pull out my phone and make the call as I hear Risk chuckle.

An hour later, after having the tables setup out back by the young prospects, Maddie is placing table cloths over top.

"We don't need tablecloths," I try to tell her. I am stopped when she turns to me abruptly with her hands on her hips, leaning forward with utter indignation in her tone.

"We are not having our friends for a meal without setting the table. Meals are a way of sharing and I want our family to feel welcome." She turns back to the table and continues to place plates, glasses, mugs, cutlery, and napkins.

The view is wreaking havoc on my dick. Each time she stretches across the table to set a place setting her heart shaped ass is on display. I want to strut up behind her, tear her shorts down and plow my dick right into her tight sheath. My thoughts are interrupted by my Pride members walking about the property in groups, enjoying the Maddie & War show as we indulge in playful banter.

"Keep that attitude, little lady, and I will be happy to smack that ass later tonight when we're alone," I let her know.

Her back straightens and she prances right over to me, raises to her tip toes while placing her hand to my jaw and kisses the corner of my mouth. "Promises, promises," she announces. And as quickly as she appeared, she disappears into the house to gather more for the table. She is definitely set for a spanking. I feel like a raunchy fourteen-year-old boy getting his first taste of a hot girl.

I force myself back to the task at hand—the most essential and accurate locations for the cameras and sensors.

This has been a productive day. My brothers spent the day making our place a virtual fortress to set my mind at ease, knowing that Maddie will be safe here.

They worked hard, and I'm forced to endure the ribbing from them all, explicitly remembering all the times I called them pussies for taking up with a woman seriously, claiming it would never happen to me. At the end of the day, they're all pleased for me and I'm glad I was able to find someone as sweet as Maddie.

Ava, Vi and Maddie spend the majority of the time indoors. Intermittently, I can hear the laughter and giggles of the "Lady Pride" as Ava likes to refer to them. Every so often Ava runs outside to ask if she can redecorate. Guard cuts that short as soon as the words leave her lips. He reminds her that she has her own house to redecorate and to stay off her feet or he's taking her home.

I check in with Maddie. I take her aside and let her know that this is our home now and she can change anything she wants as long as she doesn't get rid of anything before speaking with me.

"This is your home too. Feel free to make it a space we will both be happy with," I tell her.

She tilts her head to one side, "I like things as they are. I already feel at home."

"I want to see you living in my space. All parts of you in our home. Don't pick a corner and think that's where you belong. I want you in every room. Am I making myself clear?" I ask firmly.

"Clear," she says with a glint in her eye, "Now do you want me to tell Ava and Vi that we don't need to remodel the guest rooms or master bath? They think it's too masculine." I can hear the two trouble-makers making plans at the kitchen table.

"Guard, Orion! Get your women under control." I roar as I stalk back into the yard.

Later that evening, Maddie lounges on our bed, totally sated. Her eyes closed, lips slightly parted, expelling deep breaths; her body curves into me with her head nestled in the crook of my arm. I am almost as exhausted as my woman.

I pounced the second the last bike roared to life and left our drive, veering onto the main road. I hoisted Maddie over my shoulder in a fireman's hold, playfully slapping her ass as she shrieked with excitement all the way to the bedroom.

I made love to her slowly, building her desire and desperation for me. She moaned so sweet and begged so nicely for my cock, but I was far too entranced by exploring every crevice of her pretty pussy. I licked and sucked and lapped at her clit, stopping her from toppling into a frenzied orgasm by slowly things down and then revving her back up. I slapped her clit playfully sending another jolt of need as a long treacherous groan of frustration sounded loudly throughout the room.

I rose from between her legs, ready to plunge into her heat when Maddie sat back on her knees and before I had a minute to process, she pushed me back against the pillows, licking her way across my ribs and down my stomach all the while gripping and pumping my cock in her hands. Then that pretty pink tongue flicked the tip, licking it like an ice cream cone, paying special attention to the slit then rolling her tongue round and round the massive head until it glistened.

I grunted with an immense need to fill her mouth. She seemed to understand, taking me further into her mouth sucking gently on the tip. She moaned, sliding me in until I hit the back of her throat. I held her hair back with a hand and watched as she licked, laved, and sucked. She worked my cock until I was grunting, and it was taking a supreme effort to hold myself steady without thrusting into her mouth.

I turned her body so that she still had purchase of my cock and I had an open view of her glorious pussy. I pulled her hips down and bit gently on her clit before sucking on it hard. Maddie moaned and rocked her hips against my face. I slapped her ass and felt her pussy gush with wetness. "Suck my cock, Kitten, just like a kitty should," I said as I slapped that ass once more on her other cheek.

She took me deep and bobbed her head up and down. I moaned against her clit and kept sucking. I held her down against my mouth, knowing I wouldn't be able to hold on much longer. I insert a finger into her channel and continue to flick her clit. Her body spasmed with an intense orgasm, removing her mouth from my cock.

Her hand still held my cock and I placed mine over hers. Together we finished me off. I grunted my release as my flow spurted over my stomach.

After I cleaned up, I returned to bed with Maddie quickly coming over to pin with her arm at my waist and a leg thrown over mine.

I fall asleep, comforted by the knowledge that Maddie is all moved in and I'm keeping her safe.

CHAPTER 13

I Can be a Biker Babe

Maddie

"Ava and Vi have invited me for coffee today. We are going to Molly's where Vi works," I say as I pull my hair back into a ponytail at the nape of my neck. I lift my gaze to meet War's in the mirror and find a scowl on his face.

"I have to get to the shop today, Maddie. I can't take you in," he replies.

I giggle, "That's fine. Boys aren't allowed anyway," I tell him.

"No, Maddie, you have someone with you at all times," he says.

I turn away from the mirror to face him directly, "What? Ava and Vi don't have a babysitter following every move they make." I am becoming a little miffed. I was looking forward to time with my friends. I really enjoyed their company and I haven't had a lot of girl time. Not even when I was younger in school. My parents were ridiculously strict and had a problem with any girlfriends I brought around, so I stopped bringing them by and eventually it was too hard to maintain friendships.

"You're wrong about them not having babysitters. They do," he challenged. "You really think that Guard is going to let his pregnant wife out of his sight? And don't let Orion fool you, he has eyes on Vi too." He walks over to stand toe-to-toe with me, doing our thing, brow to brow. "I don't want anything happening to you and everything is new to you. I would feel better being with you." He is being sweet, and his concern is touching.

I bite my lip. "I promised. I don't want to break my word. These are the first friends I have met that don't care about backstage passes or how many albums we've sold. They aren't trying to get to Paul through me. They like *me*." I stress the last phrase because I want him to understand how important this is to me. "I want to live a normal life again. I am happy when I am with you and happy with them." I use my best sweet voice and wrap my arms around his waist, looking up at him, "Please?"

He looks to the ceiling then back down to me. "Okay, Baby. But not without a man nearby." He pulls my ponytail. "You wait until I can organize something, though I'm positive Guard has already done that." He pulls back to stand in the doorway. "This does not bode well for me. I look at that beautiful face and I want to give you everything. The one thing I will not compromise on is your safety, Kitten, so heed my words, you will do as you're told when I or any of the other guys is looking out for you."

He turns on his heel and walks away, pulling the phone from his back pocket. I resume applying my lip gloss. It's the only makeup I can't live without. If I am not on stage, I prefer some light blush, a little mascara and of course, my strawberry lip gloss. I catch my reflection in the mirror and notice I'm smiling. I haven't genuinely smiled or felt this good in a long time.

My shoulders are straight and strong; I have a bounce in my gait. I am more animated and share my experiences so much more. I am comfortable around War's Pride brothers and their adorable women. They treat me as an equal. Not someone broken or shattered. I would go so far as to say Risk acts like a big brother. Not the same as Paul but protective with a ton of teasing. I like when he shares that I have made War laugh more in the time we've been together he's laughed in the span of time Risk has known him. I share with Risk too. I tell him how much they all scared me at the concert and that I was so freaked out I had to hum to keep my mind occupied. I laugh about it now, knowing how silly I was to think the worst and how lucky I am to be able to call them friends.

I lived through a horrible attack, but I will not allow that act of cruelty to define my future. I have never spoken about that night. At first it was because I blocked it from my memory. I wasn't ready to deal with it and my body supressed the memory until I could cope better. Then I began to remember bits and pieces of the darkness that took away my faith in happy endings.

When he'd held me captive, I felt dirty. He called me a whore, accusing me of teasing him and playing men against one another.

"Breathe," I remind myself, "It's over. He can't hurt you anymore." I am not that weak person anymore. I am strong and resilient. I am the me I choose to be.

I slip out into the main room to find War and Cris waiting for me. "Cris is taking you, Maddie. He is picking up Ava and Vi along the way. He'll stay outside the coffee shop, so you three trouble-makers have privacy," he teases. Then in a serious tone and with great emphasis he commands, "Do. Not. Leave. The. Shop. Without. Him." I have more people guarding me now than when we actually performed, I'm about to tell him, but the thought is broken as he continues.

"Vi can be a little too independent and likes to go out exploring. You do NOT go with her. As a matter of fact, you call me, and we get a handle on her. Ava understands and wouldn't want to upset Guard. She won't be an issue."

I feel I should interject with reason, then decide to wait until he's finished.

"I have no reason to believe there will be problems, but when you agreed to be with me you also agreed to let me protect you as I see fit and I am bloody well going to do just that. Got it?" War asks, but really, he's not asking, merely stating, and I'm expected to agree.

I notice his hard jawline and determined pose and the hard set look in his eyes. I walk to him and placed my hand on his chest. He immediately covers it with his. "I know you worry, and I appreciate that you want me safe. I am not going to intentionally do something to make you upset. I promise I won't leave without Cris and will keep Vi entertained to stop her from going off on her own," I say with care. War has taken great pains to make me comfortable, the least I can do is make it as easy as possible.

Coffee with the girls is sublime. I laugh harder than ever. Vi is so animated and lively and so funny that my guts hurt from laughing so hard. We talk about the evolution of Guard and Ava. It's such a sweet and unique story that an ex-model-now-dance-teacher from New York and an MC Alpha badass president fell in love. Such different pasts but they make it work beautifully and seamlessly. They fit in each other's lives despite their differences.

Vi's story was a typical "boy meets girl, girl falls in love with bad boy biker and they live a quiet life together" one. She is much more protective of their time together, keeping an intimate piece of their lives away from everyone else that only they can share and cherish. I will say that each time Orion is mentioned her face becomes soft and gentle.

As always when girls get together, the topic of fashion and shopping comes up. I loved the tee that Ava is wearing and have to get one. "Where did you get your Harley tee?" I ask. "I didn't know Harley made maternity clothes and you are totally rocking that top. And Vi, you look killer in that red and grey Tee. I want something like that."

"Then let's move out!" Vi exclaims in excitement. "The shop is just down the street. They have the best selection of chic biker bitch wear. Last time I was in there they had the sexiest pair of biker boots. I may have to cave and buy them." She calls out to Millie for the bill, getting ready for our shop-a-thon.

The girls aren't kidding when they say the shop is just down the street. It is actually only three doors down. Cris stays behind us, watching all around, us on high alert.

I try on a Harley t-shirt dress. It is so cute. It's basically a fitted t-shirt that goes down to my knees with little cap sleeves, all in pink with a Harley logo across the chest and an inscription in white on the back stating, "Biker Chicks are Fabulous". I love it the instant I see it and can't take it off after I tried it on. Ava beams with excitement, clapping her hands when she sees it on and buys one for herself for after the baby is born. She decides on the black with red text. Vi is on a mission to find perfect accessories for each of us, including boots. She has quite the eye for jewelry and seems to have exceptional taste.

By the time we leave, I'm wearing my fabulous new dress, a pair of drop earrings in black with delicate pink flowers etched into them, a matching bangle bracelet, and to finish off the ensemble, Vi found a sexy pair of ankle boots with three-inch heels. The strap is a fine metal chain that wraps around the boot and emphasizes the ankle and calf.

Our soldier and protector, Cris, is waiting patiently. A grin spreads across his face when he sees me. "I see War is in for a nice surprise."

"This is for me," I tell him.

"Not sure he's going to want to have you wearing that when he is not around, but I am sure glad I got to see that outfit," he teases. He then proceeds to tell us that he was called back to the club and needs to know where we wanted to be dropped off.

Vi tells him that she needs to get to work. "Millie's waiting for me so she can get home. I'm closing tonight."

"Right, we'll drop you off first," he says.

"It's only a few doors down, I am sure that nothing can happen in 50 feet," Vi replies.

"Vi, I need to do my job. Don't make this hard. Let me make sure you're safe."

"Fine," she responds throwing her hands up in the air to surrender as she walks back to the shop. Cris inspects the patrons of the coffee house and turns to Vi, "Do not leave here without informing Orion. He will lose his fucking mind," he warns.

Vi raises her eyebrow and I can tell she wants to ask more questions but holds her tongue. I know she won't want to get Cris in trouble. "I will text him or call when I'm done." She gives us both hugs and thanks us for girl time. As we turn to leave, I glance back, and her expression seems a little sad and lost. I think that we should plan another girl excursion and this time concentrate on our sassy Vi and what she needs.

Ava is next to be dropped off. We leave her at the parts store that she often visits to see Guard. He is waiting for her just outside the main doors, then comes over to the jeep to help her out. He glances my way and gives me a "Hey" that reaches down to my soul along with the unofficial biker chin lift. This man is seriously hot. Not as beautiful as my guy, but definitely biker gorgeous. The way he ever so gently guides his wife from the jeep and into his arms makes me melt.

His "Kiss me Ava" is almost as sexy as, "My Kitten".

Guard turns to Chris stating, "Take Maddie to the mechanic shop. War is waiting for her there."

Cris smirks, "This is going to be good," he says and nods over to me. Guard gives me a once over as well and smiles.

"Yeah, I'm sorry I'm not going to be around for this," he says with laughing eyes.

I look from one to the other. What the heck is this all about? I glance over to Ava and can tell she is tired. I guess all that walking about has done her in, so she is no help at all in translating the biker speak.

I shrug my shoulders. "Is there something that either one of you would like to elaborate on?"

"Nope," they both say in unison. Guard leads Ava away and Cris shakes his head while making his way back around to the driver's side. Well I've had enough. "I want to know what's going on," I tell him, "Do you think War is going to be upset because we took too long?"

"He won't care about that," he states.

"Then what?" I ask forcefully.

"Maddie, you're dressed like that walking into his mechanic shop, how do you think he's going to react?" he says, continuing to focus on the road.

"I think I look nice," I say quietly, I am beginning to have doubts and maybe Ava and Vi were just being kind.

"Dressed like a biker's dream," he murmurs then more loudly interjects, "You do, Maddie, too nice," he stresses the word "nice" in a drawn-out drawl.

"Too nice?" I question. We pull into the courtyard. Cris opens my door and walks me through to the open bay. I see two legs sticking out from under an old Mustang, all black with a blur stripe running across the side. It's a hot car. The legs sticking out are even hotter. I recognize those thighs. I can see those toned, defined muscles through the material of the jeans he wars.

I don't get a word out before Cris announces, "Brought you a present, bro." I turn my head and gave Cris my fiercest "what the hell is wrong with you?" stare.

War rolls out from beneath that retro muscle car. His eyes roam the pavement and with hawk like precision, slide up from my hot biker boots to my face.

"Hi, Honey," my voice comes out husky. His stare penetrates right through me and I find myself breathless. He doesn't reply, just continues to stare. After what seems forever, he launches himself up and prowls to me holding his body taunt and tense.

I jolt out of my stupor and look around at the congregation of other eyes. Several men that I recall from the gathering at the house and the night of the concert. What seemed like an eternity was merely seconds and War is on me. His hands stretched out to pull me hard into him so that our bodies collide with force. In my bemused state, I look up as one hand glides down over my ass gripping it tight to his body, so I can feel his erection. The other hand tilts my head back further and his mouth comes down over mine in a dominating kiss. And I do mean dominating. Lips, tongue and teeth collide with mine in what's almost an out-of-body experience. I lose myself in his arms. I grip his shoulder tightly, desperate to hold myself up and press myself into him, to somehow fuse our connection for eternity.

His head pulls back, and our lips disconnect, and I whimper in protest. My eyes flutter open to focus on those magnificent swollen lips that have just plundered mine which I assume are just as puffy. His eyes are still smoldering with desire. I endeavour to lighten the mood, considering we are at his place of business.

"Do you like my dress?" I ask breathlessly, still holding onto him until my legs are ready to hold me steady.

War blinks his eyes for a spilt second and with arms wrapped around my waist, cinching me tight, turns his head back and lets out a roar of laughter. It's so beautiful when he laughs that I can't help but join in.

"Yeah, Baby, I love your dress." He gives me a little squeeze then growls right into my ear, "I like it so much I want to lift the skirt to your waist, rip your panties off, and fuck you hard on the hood of that car until you beg me to stop."

I let out a muted, "*Oh*", licking my lips, letting him know I would be good with that. It would have to wait though, as we still have an audience. "We have company," I remind him.

"Yes, we certainly have," he lets out an exasperated sigh and struts along the pavement to the back of the bay stopping at the sweet ride he was working on, tugging me along with him. He releases me long enough to drop the hood of the car, reaches in to take the keys from the ignition then reaches back tagging my hand to a room that's probably an office. He drops the key off on the counter just outside the door. Yet another tattooed biker hottie with dark eyes and a bald head sits behind the counter, looking up from what he's working on to see War and me. I smile and say a quick, "Hi." He lifts his chin in greeting.

War jerks his head towards the keys. "Rod can come pick up his car. I've listed the parts and labour on the clipboard. I'm going to finish up the paperwork in my office. I don't want to be disturbed."

The door closes behind us and I turn my head back to see War leaning back against it, arms and legs crossed with a sultry smile on his lips. "Baby, do you think it was wise to come here and tease me with that dress?" he asks as he moves across the room to the chair behind the desk.

"I didn't wear this dress to tease you," I gasp. How could he think I would be a tease? "If you think for one minute that I would do that then you don't know me at all."

Suddenly, I feel my mind shut down. I can't breathe, my heart is beating so fast I feel it's going to explode from my chest. I see the letters spread out all over the floor. Those awful letters from that madman with all those horrible lies. I was a cock tease and deserved to be punished. He was going to find me and make me his good girl again. He was coming for me because I was a tease. I was a bad girl doing bad things and he was coming for me. I freeze in fright. My heart hammering against my chest so hard I'd swear It could be heard from a block away. I can't breathe. My head starts to spin. Strong arms grab me, but I fight him. I pull at his arms, scratching and clawing at his hands as I am placed in a bear-like grip as I scream. Maybe someone will hear me this time. I shriek as loud as I can. Someone will save me if they can hear me. They will come for me.

"Shh! Baby, stop. You're going to hurt yourself. Stop. It's me, Baby. It's Xander, Kitten. I'm here. You're safe," a quiet voice whispers in my ear.

The door is thrown open ferociously and hits the wall with a bang. Cris and Risk are at the forefront followed by a platoon of others. They came running for me. The men's first instinct is to ensure our safety. I barley look at them. I feel a hand on my cheek turning my head. I meet memorable eyes. I know those eyes.

"Breathe, Baby, nice and slow." I must be responding because he continues, "That's it, Kitten." War directs me until I'm back in control and am able to focus on him and our surroundings. "Look at me, Baby, it's me. I'm here." I blink up at him and my eyes fill with tears. I let loose in his arms as he cradles me gently.

I hear War's voice as he holds me close. "I've got her, guys. You can go back to work."

I feel like I have been crying for hours and I'm totally exhausted. I hiccup and murmur, "I'm so sorry." I place my hands over my face; I am so embarrassed.

"Baby, what happened?" he asks as his eyes meet mine.

"You…you called me a tease. And…uh…" I couldn't go on and instead look for the quickest escape route.

"Kitten, I was playing with you." He forces me to meet his eyes. "You look beautiful in that dress. I could barely keep my hands off you. I am a lucky man to have you with me." He pauses to let that information penetrate. "I caution to bring this up Maddie, but it's obvious I triggered something. I don't want to push you to tell me unless you're ready, however, the more I am aware of what happened, the better I can help get us through this."

I haven't spoken to anyone about it. The details of that night have remained solely with me. Not even Paul knows the whole story. I have tried so hard to bury it and forget. I want to tell War, but I am so afraid he'll judge me or blame me for what happened. What if he can't handle my past?

On the other hand, I want a real relationship. That means trusting War with the greatest fears that I have lived through. I deserve normalcy, a full life, and to have that, I need to tell him everything.

"What if you can't handle what I tell you?" my voice trembles. "What if you think I deserved…" I don't finish that sentence because one look at his face and I see a flash of anger as his hand tightens on my knee.

"I am not him," he states firmly.

"I'm not saying you are," I counter. "I know you aren't him. You are the most wonderful man I have ever met, and I don't want to change what we have." I reach out to caress his face.

"Babe, change can be good. Life is all about change and growth. That doesn't mean we can't do that together. You need to trust me with this, so we can work it out and get you to the other side, knowing I'm going to stand by you." His lips touch mine lightly.

I climb off his lap and move to sit on the two-seater couch in the room. I pat the seat next to me, encouraging War to join. "I am going to tell you everything. Please don't interrupt, just let me get it all out." I clasp my hands tightly on my lap.

"I love to sing. It makes me feel alive and that I have a special gift that I can contribute. The lyrics I write are about beauty, love and tragedy too. When I create, I feel connected to people because music is a universal language. When I perform, I am adding actions to the words I sing. What I didn't realize was that my words and actions are subjective to the listener. My understanding and feelings are mine and everyone else, although hearing the same words, interpret them in their own way." I stood to pace the room.

"One day I started getting fan mail from this one fan in particular. I would get a new note every day. I was flattered at first. They were pretty harmless. He wrote about how much he liked my music and loved my voice. He went on to say that I was the most beautiful angel he had ever seen. I never replied, partly because I didn't have the time and Paul thought it was a little creepy that he was writing so many letters." I shrug my shoulders and stretch out my hands. "I don't know what changed. The letters started becoming harsh. He didn't like what I wore at my last concert, or the way I wore my hair. He commented that I spoke salaciously to someone in the audience. He actually wrote that—*salaciously*. As Paul heard more, we came together, the whole band, and decided to step up security, not that we were sure that he would be a threat, but we were getting more coverage and were therefore more popular and thought it was the smart thing to do." I force back tears. "I didn't know how sick he was. I wasn't trying to lead him on."

"Baby," War rumbles.

"No. Stop. Let me get it all out." I raise my hand up palm out to stop him from coming to me. "Let me finish." He nods, and I continue.

"The letters stopped coming a week before the concert. I assumed that he found someone else more interesting and, in this industry, there is a new star rising all the time. We had good security and they took great lengths to ensure we were safe. I don't know how he got back stage. I don't know how he managed to drug the entire band. I was sitting in my dressing room, waiting for the crowds to thin so we could all go home. Paul and I have a ritual of getting nachos and root beer after a show. I love that moment together with him. It was all we could afford after our first gig and it's what we've done ever since." I smile at the memory.

Then I drag out a long breath. "The door was pushed open violently and there he was with a gun in his hand. I had no idea who he was at first and then he said he was there to save me. That's when I knew it was him. I started to call out for Paul and the others, but he dragged me to where they were. They were passed out, but at the time, he told me he'd poisoned them, and they were dead." I caught my breath. War reached out to hold my hand. "He said it was my fault. They turned me into a slut and he needed to make me clean. I cried and ran towards my brother, but he grabbed me and dragged me across the room and out the door. He said if I made any sound or movement to alert anyone, he would shoot them dead and I would be to blame for their deaths too."

I squeeze War's fingers. "He threw me into a car. I tried to talk to him and tell him I needed to get back to my family and friends. I wanted to reason with him and make him see me as a regular person and he got more and more angry and hit me hard with his fist. He told me I was his family now, then I must have passed out. When I come to, my face ached, and I had a horrible headache. I can remember holding my cheek and forcing my eyes shut because the light was too bright. When I was finally able to focus, I saw that I was in a basement. He gave me a sandwich, but my jaw hurt too much, and I was so terrified, I couldn't eat. He ranted that I was an ungrateful little bitch. It went on for hours about how they'd tainted his angel and he needed to get her back. Over and over and over.

I had to sit down again for the next part but forced myself to look directly at War. "He told me to undress. He needed to get me clean." I cleared my throat. "I refused, and he hit me again. He asked me again and again. I refused each time and each time he hit me. Then he started ripping at my clothes. I fought as hard as I could. Then he threw me against the wall and I crumbled to the floor. He kicked me over and over while he screamed, 'Whore leave her body'. I thought I was going to die. And truth be told, I wanted to die. I thought Paul was dead and it was all my fault." I start sobbing quietly. War reaches out; I hold him off.

"He stopped kicking me when I couldn't move anymore. He pulled me into his arms while I was bleeding and crying. He tells me that he killed the whore inside me and I can be his angel again. I don't know how I found the strength to pull away and curl into a ball in the corner of the room." I wipe the tears from my cheeks. "The door burst open then and all I could see was cops rushing in. He screamed that he won't let them taint me again and will kill me first. I wanted it to end and I didn't care if I died. Everyone I loved was dead and I just didn't care anymore. I closed my eyes and waited for the end. The next thing I knew, the cops had disarmed him, and I was carried out to an ambulance and taken to the hospital."

I take War's hand and hold on tight. "When Paul walked in, I was in shock. I thought he was dead, and apparently, I completely lost it after that. They had to sedate me. They wanted to take my clothes and all I could feel was his hands on me. Paul held and rocked me and until I was calm, and I agreed to let the doctors work on me."

I'm afraid to meet War's gaze full-on. Does he think I'm dirty too? Or worse, will I find a look of pity because I was too weak to fight harder, to break away?

His hand slides under my chin, and I can't ignore his gaze any longer. But I don't see pity or hate. I see anger.

"You are not to blame for any of it. Not. One. Damn. Thing," War states. "When I look at you, I see a woman that cared more for others than for herself. I see strength and resilience. You are talented, beautiful, and strong. You are a survivor and as long as I live, I promise you will never have to fight, and if for some reason you do, I will fight alongside of you." He moves my hand to his chest; I can feel his heart beating strong.

"He called me dirty. A whore. Unclean. He said my lyrics were offensive and sexual and were leading people into depravity. I thought I was responsible for my brother's death. I thought my friends were lost to me," I sob quietly again his chest. "I just want to make music that everyone enjoyed. I want to sing."

When I finally pull my head from his chest to look up, his eyes are glazed with tears; he's absorbing my pain. "I refuse concerts because I'm afraid. I'm afraid for me, but I'm also afraid for my family. I don't want anyone else to get hurt. I don't know that I can ever recover from something like that. It took me a long time to even be able to record again. I went back to the studio to prove to myself that I was healing. I was taking a piece of myself back."

My lip began to tremble, and I forced myself to continue, "When you called me a tease, I heard his voice in my head. All the horrible words he called me, and those letters filled with hate crawled through my mind like a toxic serpent slithering around me ready to strike." I place my hands on either side of his face and beg him, "Please don't give up on me. I am try-ing to get this all under control. Please just give me more time." My bottom lip quivers and as much as I try to stop it, I can't.

He lifts me into his lap, "I am not going anywhere, and neither are you. We are going to get through this together. I am so proud of you; you fought hard to get to this place with me and now I am telling you that you are not alone." A sweet kiss on my brow and then one on my nose. I am not alone I can feel it down to my bones.

I give a small smile, but it disappears when I see War's lips thin. "I need to know Maddie. I need to know if he touched you—I mean intimately. I want to know so we can work through this together and so

I can be more aware of how to handle you with care," he said. He struggles to ask me, and I wonder if it's because he isn't sure he wants to know the truth.

I hold on tight to him and answer, "I fought him with everything I had in me. Each time he tried to kiss me, I would flinch, turn, or push him away. When he started to get more violent, he didn't want to touch me that way because he thought I was a whore. I preferred the beating to him touching me. I would have preferred death to his touch."

"You are the strongest woman I know. Brave and smart with the voice of an angel." War strokes my hair and kisses my jaw.

"They all could have died because of me, War. I would have been to blame," I tell him.

"Bullshit! That sick fuck is to blame and no one else. NOT YOU. NEVER YOU!" His voice filled with anger. War squeezes me a little and softens his tone. "I don't want you to ever think that again. I am the luckiest man and every one of the guys outside in that shop came running in here to protect you because they agree that I have something very special in my arms."

I smile broadly and lighten the mood. "I think I can be a biker chick," I say as I run a hand down my dress.

That sexy huge smile crosses his face, "Yeah, Baby, you are going to be a great biker chick."

CHAPTER 14

Something's Missing

War

It takes all my strength to control my temper in front of my brothers. That dumb fuck is going to pay for what he did to Maddie. When I find him, I am going to make sure he never gets another opportunity to terrorize her again.

Some would say he is mentally ill and needs help. I'm not willing to take any chances.

The guys are curious about what went down with Maddie. We are going to have to step up our game and find him soon. I want to be able to tell Maddie she can breathe and live free. Knowing he is out there, lurking, has me more than a bit concerned. I have an internal battle going on inside as to whether to alert Maddie that this guy is out there and has been around her apartment.

I leave Maddie jotting notes on a page and strumming her guitar. I walk onto the deck to place a call to Guard.

"Hey, man," Guard answers.

"Hey", I reply. "Maddie has filled in all the holes in her story. We are dealing with one sick fuck." I sigh heavily into the hone while running a hand over my head and down across my neck. "I think we need to meet up and give the brothers the details, so we know what we're dealing with," I finish.

"Jesus, Christ! That doesn't sound good." Guard's gruff voice huffs out.

"Not good at all. Cris and Risk saw her freak out first-hand today. An explanation will express just how dire this situation is, but more importantly they need to know this man is *twisted*. I need someone on Maddie for when you call this meeting."

"Cris?" he asks.

"I want him at the meeting. He saw her. He gets how bad it is. How about Demon? Then you or I can fill him in later,"

"Sure, that works. I'll set it up for tonight and have him come by," Guard confirms.

I snap my phone shut as I make my way back inside the house.

Maddie is still sitting cross-legged on the over-sized leather chair in the corner, guitar in hand, strumming and humming like she doesn't have a care in the world. It's like the last two hours never happened. I, however, will never forget her ear-piercing scream. The tears streaming down her face in utter terror. I will probably have nightmares thinking of her helpless with that demented psychopath.

"That's sounds real pretty, Baby." I tell her softly.

She glances up, her fingers still wrapped around the neck of the guitar, "I think a new song is forming." Her smile is brilliant.

"What's it called?" I ask as I approach her.

"Not there yet. But when I play it reminds me of sunrises." She places the guitar beside her, leaning on the side of the chair and stretches out her hand. She tugs me onto the chair and makes her way onto my lap, securely nestled as she wraps her arms around my neck. "I will be sure to keep you in the loop," she whispers.

"Kitten, today was pretty intense. Are you good?" I am anxious and want to make sure that she is handling all that she shared with me.

She pauses and then nods her head firmly, stating, "I'm good."

"Convince me," I tell her, ensuring we keep eye contact.

A genuine shy smile forms on her perfect bow lips as she says, "I'm here with you. I have good friends. I am healthy and strong. I am more the me I want to be each and every day that passes and I am happy. Really, truly happy." Our foreheads touch in our signature move. "Now you need to know that I am going to work really hard at not letting the past determine our future. I want to be with you and I love how we fit together."

I place my mouth over hers. I kiss her slowly, exploring her taste and savouring the feel of her lips on mine. "I'm happy too, Kitten. Never thought I would feel this way with someone. You are incredible, Baby. Never forget it," I tell her.

"Roger that, Captain," she teases.

"I love your smart mouth, Baby, keep that up and you'll get that spanking I've been promising you," I tease back. Maddie rolls her eyes. "Tell you what," I continue, "keep on keeping on with your creative juices flowing and I will grill some steaks for dinner."

"I can help," she immediately offers. I keep her steady in my lap.

"No, Baby, you cooked last night. Tonight, you make beautiful music. My turn to make dinner. Although I will tell you, I am not making salad. You'll get a baked potato and steak," I confirm.

"Greens are good for you, Honey," she says with a giggle.

"Yeah, but I don't make salads, so you're getting a baked potato," I reiterate.

She glides her hands over my shoulders, "I love baked potato," then quickly adds, "and steak and mostly I love that you are making it for me. So, thank you."

I wish that I could stay like this all night, but I have a woman to feed and I have to devise a plan to get rid of this dark cloud looming over us by catching that asshole. "Let me up, babe. Let me feed my girl."

I inform Maddie that Demon is coming to stay with her and give her a heads up on his quiet quirk. "Baby, he doesn't say much. Don't be offended, it's just his way. Go about doing what you do; he is coming to keep an eye on things."

"Why does he have to come at all? I'm sure everyone from the other clubs have completely forgot about me."

I decide not to inform her of the possible peril that may be looming until I have more information from

Orion as to the whereabouts of Jefferson Hendley. I will see what tonight turns up and then make my decision. "You're probably right, but I will feel better knowing you're safe," I say.

"Fine. If it makes you feel better. I don't want you to think I need a babysitter. I did live alone for a while before we met, War. I can be alone," she reminds me.

"My tigress," I tease. "Let's just go with this for a little while longer. Just so you know, Ava and Vi need to put up with this too."

"I don't think Vi does much of what she's told," Maddie snorts.

"Orion has his ways," I tell her firmly.

Dinner is easy. Easy flowing conversation about fun stuff. I make note that her next birthday cake is going to be caramel cheesecake because it's her favourite. Demon makes an appearance and I quickly kiss Maddie goodbye and make my way to the club.

Guard calls the meeting to order. "War wants to give us some intel on Jefferson. I suggest we all listen close and save questions for the end." He turns to me. "Go ahead, brother."

I look around the room before I start. I see the curious eyes. The brothers that were at the garage are paying close attention. "A few of you saw the reaction Maddie had today, but none of you know why. I need to tell you all of it. You need to know because this will make you all more diligent and because as my brothers, there is no group of men I trust more than all of you. It makes my blood boil to rehash this again, but you all need to know the severity of the situation." I matter-of-factly state the details of the beating, the fucked-up thoughts, the horrid things that monster said and did to my woman. I tell them about the impact of the guilt she's been reliving. How she felt responsible for the deaths of everyone she loved. How she walked out into a room where everyone she cared for were passed out and how she was made to think they were dead. I tell them everything.

As the story unfolds, I can see their jaws clenching and the fists forming by their sides. An intense resounding anger echoes through the room. This is not only because it happened to Maddie but because this could have happened to any of our women.

"This guy is smart. He was able to get backstage with solid security in place. He was able to drug them all that night. He had been watching her for months and knew their routine. He had it planned perfectly. The cops got lucky with the security officer sensing a problem and taking down the car and plate number," I continued, "but we cannot rely on luck. I don't want her to ever suffer. This man will never get the opportunity to torture her again. He is smart and was able to convince his doctors that he's stable." I finish with, "I have a bad feeling in my gut. It won't go away, and it's never steered me wrong."

Guard stands up beside me. "Where do we stand with finding this guy?" he directs this question at Orion.

"Still working on it. We have been sitting in his parent's neighbourhood, but he hasn't made an appearance. He has officially skipped one of his counselling sessions, which means the cops are going to be alerted as well," he states.

"So, he is out there, and we haven't got shit," I say. I can't hide my pissy tone. "Do I tell her that Jefferson is out there, waiting to strike?"

"I will get heavier tracking through the computer. Step it up and hope he pays with a credit or debit card. See if we can get more concrete information," he suggests. I can see that Orion is frustrated. His game face is on and that means he'll be relentless until he finds him. Great news for me.

Guard pipes up, "Maybe we tell her. Could be best at this point."

"Christ, she is finally happy. She told me this is the first time in two years that she feels calm. And settled. She laughed wholeheartedly for the first time with Ava and Vi. She thinks I am being vigilant because of the other MCs and the shit that went down that night. Now I have to go home and tell her that her greatest nightmare may be back for a second go. It'll destroy her all over again." By the time I'm done, I'm shouting at the top of my lungs.

"Don't tell her yet," Risk says, raising his hands. "Hear me out. We are starting work on the studio. We can take turns supervising; giving each of us an excuse to be there every day, keeping watch. It will give us more time to find a lead."

"It's solid," says Guard.

"Yeah," I breathe out. "What about Ava and Vi? This fucker played her by leveraging her brother and friends. There is nothing to stop him from using our families to flush her out."

I notice Guard and Orion tense up. The idea of someone going after their women can't sit well.

"Ava will be spending more time with me at the parts store. I've been pushing her to stay close lately. We set up a rotation, taking turns to ensure their safety. Except Orion, I want you to focus on finding this fucker," Guard states.

"I think I should tell Vi," Orion says. "She's smart. She'll be on guard and can keep an eye open for anything out of the ordinary."

"She won't be able to keep this quiet," Guard interjects. "If she acts any differently, Ava is going pick up on that fast. Those two read each other's minds."

Orion's voice is loud and firm, "If I am out there hunting, then she is alone and exposed. She already knows something' up." Orion is right about Vi. She knows this club and she picks up on our shit.

"Check her work schedule. See if we can get Millie to keep her there longer. Then we will just need to follow her there and back. You can work your operation from home. Cris will help with the setup, so you can be close by at night. Any street work goes to Demon and some of the other brothers. Risk, you stay with the crew at War's place and keep an eye on Maddie. If Demon needs help, we will call on you." Guard looks at Orion. "That work for you?"

Orion nods, "Yeah, I can make that work."

"When we get this guy, I want the first shot at him," I tell Guard.

"You got it," Guard confirmed.

With the wheels in motion and a plan in place, I am in a better place. I am stepping up to my front door when I hear Maddie talking. "Are you sure you didn't throw it in with your stuff?"

I can see that she is listening attentively to whoever is on the other end.

Maddie goes on, "It doesn't make sense. I always keep that photo album in that box. You know how particular I am about order. It's not there and I've opened every box."

Maddie continues to focus on her call and nods.

"Okay, I'll keep looking," she mumbles.

A heavy sigh.

"If I can't find it, I'll go back to my place and check. Can I go to your apartment and look? Just in case it got caught up in your things?" Then, "I won't worry, and I'll keep looking. Love you, big brother."

Finally, I enter. Demon is sitting by an open box and glares up at me as I approach. I look at him knowing exactly what he is trying to say. I move towards Maddie.

"Hey, Kitten, how was your night?" I ask nonchalantly.

"Um, good," she says off-handedly. Her mind is on something else entirely.

"What's going on?" I ask, taking care to remain casual.

"I can't find my photo album," she says. Her arms are folded under her breasts and I can see that she is thinking hard on this.

"I'm sure it will turn up," I tell her.

"You're probably right. It just doesn't make any sense. I always put it with my journals," she says as she looks up at me. "Maybe it was left at my apartment?"

I look over at Demon. He and Cris were in charge of getting Maddie's stuff packed and moved. He shakes his head firmly. I know there's more to this and I need to get some time alone with Demon.

"Not that I know of, Maddie. I will send someone to look though. Why don't you go check the other box again?" I urge her, guiding my hand at the small of her back out the door to the spare room where we placed all her boxes.

I wait for her to be out of earshot and catch Demon jerking his head, motioning for me to move closer to him. He points to the box and fingers the journals all lined up in a row, spines facing out with start and end dates on display. One is missing. A quick calculation in my head brings me to the year that Jefferson was away in the institution. I reach out to grab one of the books only to have Demon stop me. I look at him, he wiggles his fingers. I get it, he wants to check for prints. We know who they belong to but making it all stick in a court of law means gathering all the information.

Jefferson is closer than I expected. Thank God, I have Maddie in my house. The stalker was in her apartment.

"Gotta tell Guard and Orion," I tell Demon. He nods. "Keep her distracted if she comes back."

"It's not there, War. I checked," she says as she walks back into the room, moving straight towards the open box near Demon. Demon raises a hand and points to the kitchen. Maddie quirks her eyebrow, "Now you want pie?" she asks. She looks stern yet fuckably cute.

Demon puts on the performance of a lifetime with his innocent smile and bauble-head dog in the car window.

"Okay! Okay!" she blathers. "Coffee and pie." She continues as she walks to the kitchen, "All night I ask if he wants coffee, tea, pie, chips and dip, and all he does is shake his head. And now, he doesn't even ask. Nope, he just points to the kitchen…"

I have blocked the view of Demon working on getting an imprint. The man has mad skills. I turn my head toward him to check on his progress and he nods that he is done for now. I know that he is going to have to take a closer look and I have to get this box out of the way before she compromises any prints by adding more of her own, or notices that one journal is missing.

"Babe, I am going to move this box into the spare room before we trip over it."

"Kay, I guess I'll look again tomorrow," she replies.

"Just wait. I'll send someone to make sure we didn't forget anything," I said, "Might as well let it go until I can check it out."

Demon has moved the box out of the way and is sitting on the couch waiting for pie by the time Maddie emerges with a tray in hand. He takes a bite of his pie and moans in appreciation. Maddie laughs and splutters, "That's the most he's said to me all night." She laughs louder. It's contagious and I find myself laughing as well.

Demon takes full advantage of the situation, finishing off his pie before tearing into mine.

A little while after Demon leaves, I walk out of the bathroom to find a sexy vision of Maddie sitting in bed humming and writing in her notebook. I place one hand on the bed and one behind her head, guiding her to meet me halfway where our lips touch lightly. She then scans my body, her eyes lingering on the towel draped around my waist and licks her lips. A wicked smile forms on her glorious face. My siren rises to her knees, kissing my chest then abdomen, moving lower still as she unwraps the towel. Soft hands take my cock and grip it firmly. My cock is rock hard at her touch. Maddie looks down hungrily, continuing to stroke it lovingly. She boldly licks the tip, lapping at my pre-cum, swirling her tongue around and around. She moans in appreciation and begins to lick the full length of me. The heat of her mouth is extraordinary. My back spasms and legs tense as she grows bolder, taking my full length in her mouth. I am so entranced by her eyes staring into mine as she moans deeply over my cock and begins to suckle on the tip. I know I won't last long at this rate.

"Maddie, I'm going to come, Baby," I groan.

She sucks harder taking all of me in her mouth, moving her hands magically down over my thighs to the back holding me while her mouth continues to push me closer and closer to the edge.

I warn her again, "Baby, I'm about to come." I pull lightly on her hair to let her know that I am going to explode in her mouth if she doesn't move.

"I want to taste you," she whispers and continues to suck me down. I am completely undone by those words. I can't control it any longer and release my cum in her sweet mouth. She holds my cock in her mouth until it starts to soften.

She looks very pleased with herself. "Did I do it right?" she asked.

"Any righter and I may never let you leave this room," I tell her.

I toss her onto her back pulling her to the edge of the bed until her legs dangle. I rip off her bottoms along with her panties and kneel before her, splaying her wide. "My turn," I tell her and proceed to fill the room with sounds of Maddie begging for her release.

Hours later, I am lying next to a very sated Kitten, listening to her soft breath as she sleeps. Unfortunately, my thoughts turn to the missing journal and photo album. Her stalker is out there, and he has a piece of my woman. I know he's waiting to strike; I can sense the danger looming.

CHAPTER 15

Wonder and Awe

Maddie

What is that excessive noise outside? I bury my head under the pillow to drown out the banging, dinging, and buzzing of saws.

"Babe, time to get up," War says as he lifts the hair away from my neck, kissing the spot his fingers graze.

"Too early." My muffled voice is buried in the pillow, clutching it close and I refuse to open my eyes. Maybe if I don't, they will all just shush, and I can sleep a little longer.

"Kitten, we have ten men in our yard that are going to be making a lot more noise as they start work on the studio today. We need to keep them supplied with food and coffee," he says as he pulls the covers off me. I was too tired to pull on my shorts and tank after our vigorous night exploring each other. One eye peeps open. I'm just about to tell him they should start tomorrow, when his hand slides over my thigh then hip, ending in a light slap on my ass, waking me right up.

"I see I have your full attention, Baby. The faster they get started the faster they are done. Then you can spend all the time you want in your new studio, doing what you love to do in a space that's all yours," he says. Tapping my ass again, a sly smile emerges. "If you don't get out of bed, I am going to have to find a creative way to get you out of bed."

Oh boy, that actually sounds naughty and exciting! My lips part as I lifted my head from the pillow.

"I'm going to count to three and if you're not up, I get to take matters into my own hands," War stands straight with his arms crossed and a glint of mischief in his eye.

"One," he begins. I sit up not sure if I should tempt him further. I bite my lip and watch him as he forms the number two with one hand. "Two," he says. Oh, but he looks so good posed like he is ready to strike. So sexy. "Last chance, Kitten," he growls.

"I'm not moving," I tell him. I did it. I poked the bear. Or …um…Warrior. It's exhilarating.

His fingers form the number three, then he jolts towards me with both arms, "Three!" he says as he grabs my feet and pulls me to the edge of the bed until my toes hit the floor. I eek with surprise. He bends at the waist and suddenly I'm over his shoulder and being held carefully but firmly with one hand as the other slaps my ass.

"Okay, Okay! I'll get up!" I tell him, giggling. I grip his waist to steady myself, but he lightly slaps my ass again.

"Too late, Kitten. A lesson must be taught," he says with a sinister laugh. He prowls into the bathroom and turns on the shower. He tears off my panties, unzips his jeans and steps out of them. All this without dropping me. Then he plants me on my feet in the shower and follows me in, caging me into the corner.

I am so turned on that move to jump him. He catches my hands in his. "Turn around, Baby," his voice is a low sexy groan. I do so immediately. "Hands on the wall," he commands. My heart beats faster, not in fear but in shear excitement over what he has planned. Water rains down over us, making both our bodies slick. His hands come around to my breasts and lather them lavishly. He takes great care to play with my nipples, flicking and twisting gently. His hands move over my shoulders and then back and around to my stomach, ensuring that every part of me is touched and teased. He nudges my legs apart as he continues to lather my behind, spreading me just enough to touch and explore, not forgetting a single inch of my body. I wait patiently for his hands to find my pussy. I'm so wet for him. I spread my legs further and push back against his hands, urging him to continue.

"Greedy girl," he teases as he nips my ear.

"Uh huh," is all I manage to get out. His hand slides through my folds and I'm so turned on I'm sure they can hear me from across the house. His hand flicks my clit and caresses in a circular motion. Two fingers enter me gently, while the other continues to play with my now engorged clit. I rocked myself against his hand, wanting the friction to take me over the edge. With his hands still in place and his legs holding me still, he asks against my ear, "You going to make me coffee, Kitten?"

I'll make him a seven-layer cake from scratch with fudge icing and homemade ice cream as long as he keeps doing what he's doing. "Anything you want, Honey." I tell him in a desperate plea.

"I want my Kitten to stay still as I finger fuck her, then I want to fuck her again, so I can come inside her," he murmurs in my ear.

His fingers continue their magic and I can't help myself and fall off the cliff into an orgasm.

"Not finished yet, Baby," he growls.

I moan in response, unable to respond in words.

My head tilts back to hit his shoulder, arching my back, earning me a tender bite between my shoulder and neck. I shudder in delight as he places the tip of his cock between my folds, then with one firm stroke he fills me to the hilt. I gasp at the force of his thrust, feeling him move inside me as I claw at the tile to hold myself steady. He continues to penetrate me fast and hard. I climb higher and higher towards the pinnacle of another orgasm. I didn't think I could come again so soon; War proves me wrong as I fall over that cliff again, panting for him to never stop. I revel in his growl of release, his cock filling me completely.

War waits until my breathing has returned to normal and gently pulls out, taking care to wrap his arms around me to keep me steady on my feet. He moves us under the water to rinse us both clean, shuts off the water and wraps a soft fluffy towel around me. I am lifted in his arms and deposited on the bed. I notice that he doesn't even bother covering himself. He is dripping water on the floor and looks delicious.

"Kitten, get that look off your face. I have already kept my brothers waiting. I need to go out and help them," he says as he towels off and begins getting dressed.

I come out of my stupor. "I'll get dressed and bring you all coffee and fresh muffins."

"I don't want you going into town alone," he says.

I raise a hand to stop him. "Don't worry. I plan to bake them from scratch." I smile up at him.

"Thank you, Baby. I'm sure that the guys will appreciate your efforts. I'll show you how much I appreciate your efforts later," he says with a wink.

He bends forward and places his hands on either side of my waist, kissing my lips. Then he turns and walks out the door. I could wake up like this every morning.

I head out onto the deck an hour later with round two of coffee and two dozen homemade muffins. I ask War to bring out the long table, drape a white table cloth over top and set it up buffet style with a carafe I found among my boxes in the spare room. I add raspberry and strawberry jams, butter, napkins and cutlery. I decided to make two different batches of muffins—chocolate chip and blueberry; War mentioned that his favourite was chocolate chip and I figured the blueberry would go over well. I add a platter of fresh fruit for a touch of healthy.

"Honey, come get them while they are still warm," I call out to War.

"I've been inhaling the delicious smell of muffins baking for the last half hour. I'm first," Cris runs up the steps to the table and I giggle. I take two chocolate chip muffins, cut them in half and dollop a teaspoon of raspberry jam on each side, something I saw once on the cooking channel. The raspberry and chocolate make an awesome combination.

The guys are already indulging in their breakfast when War makes his way to me. I hold out his plate to him. "Where's yours, Baby?" his smooth voice rumbles against my hair as he placed a light kiss on the top of my head.

"I'll get one after you're all done," I say. "I like to see you guys enjoying it."

"There won't be any left the way these guys are inhaling them," War replies. He isn't wrong. I glanced over at the platters and they're almost empty. Oh well, I can have toast.

"I'll have to make a big batch of chili for lunch," I say as I looked across the table to see Cris and Risk arguing over the last chocolate chip muffin. I can't help but laugh.

War chuckles too. "I guess I lucked out when my girl decided that I was worth two muffins." He takes another bite, moaning with pleasure. "Baby, these are really good." He leans down and brushes his lips against me in a light, deliciously chocolate kiss. "Thank you, Kitten." Simple words but his eyes say it all. He is happy. Happy to be together and happy to be surrounded by brothers who care.

I spend most of my day happily working in the kitchen. I fill the dishwasher with breakfast dishes, wipe counters, start a huge pot of chili and leave it to simmer. I make our bed, do a load of laundry, all very mundane stuff and yet I can't stop smiling through it all. Every time I look out the window, I notice how hard all the guys are working to make my studio. My heart grows more and more full. They barely know me and here they are building my sanctuary. The plans that Risk drew up are amazing. He truly thought of everything.

I can't wait to share my new family with Paul. I miss him but true to his word, he calls me every night and tells me all about their gigs and what's going on with the band. I tell him that I'm writing again and have some great tunes floating through my mind. Paul is thrilled that I am so happy and safe. War says that he can stay with us for a while when he gets back, so we can spend time reconnecting.

The day goes by fairly quickly. The men stop for lunch and I make fresh corn bread to go along with the chili. They wolf it down quickly then proceed to devour my coconut raspberry squares. They are the one recipe my mom made that I absolutely loved. We may not be close, but she still makes them for me when I go home at Christmas to visit. She doesn't make a big deal of it but always makes sure that I get two on my plate. It's a good thing that we have a fully stocked pantry and freezer so that I can rediscover my love of cooking and baking. In the past, I've rarely taken the time since the band is constantly eating, spending most of our time in a studio or on the road.

The soft warm wind blows through the trees. I can hear the rippling of the water in the creek. The birds are singing to us, happy, joyful chirping from the trees. War and I are sitting side by side, his hand quietly caressing mine. His other hand holds a beer bottle, while mine holds a glass of red wine. It's in this moment that I realize I have all I ever dreamed of. I'm in the presence of sheer beauty. This place, his friends, my new girlfriends, the studio they're working so hard to build, the scenery, and yet the only thing that truly means anything to me is the touch of War's hand engulfing my smaller one, squeezing it tight to get my attention. I looked into those mesmerizing eyes and am filled with wonder and awe.

I've had people chanting my name at concerts, enough money that I'll be able to retire comfortably when I choose, a brother who would die for me and has made supreme sacrifices to ensure I have all I need, and I know that I am blessed. With all that has happened, the good and the bad, I wouldn't change a thing if at the end, I can moments like this, with the man I love by my side, smiling that crooked smile beneath sparking eyes, here in our oasis.

CHAPTER 16

Play It Again

War

This last week had been a flurry of activity. The studio is almost complete. The structure is erected and solid. Risk has hand-picked each person that has come onto my property, doing background checks and ensuing Maddie's safety. We are starting the final stage; the electronic boards and equipment will be arriving tomorrow. The crew cut out early today to get ready for the Friday night party at the club house. We work hard, and we play hard. It's part of the life I chose when I became part of Satan's Pride. I was so young that all the partying seemed like the perfect life. What more can a 20-year-old want? I had booze, women, and my Pride brothers. I couldn't imagine wanting more than that. Now I stand in the doorway to living room and see Maddie strumming her guitar, fingers concentrating on the strings, brow furrowed like she's searching for the next perfect notes to play. Her hair is thrown over one shoulder exposing her creamy, silky neck, marked with my love bites.

The sight of her marked like that makes me hard all over again. I'm tempted to throw her over my shoulder and take her back to bed. I can't get enough of her. Every kiss, lick, touch is making me more and more addicted. I feel the phone buzz in my pocket before it starts to ring.

I walked away from the door to the front porch and answered. "Hey."

"Yo, brother, I got an update." Orion's deep voice penetrates through the phone.

"Right," I respond.

"Brace, brother. I found a connection and this asshole is preparing. Before I go on, is Maddie with you?" Orion asks.

"In the other room," I reply. "She fully engaged with her guitar. It would take a cannon to break that concentration." I smile because I know I could call her name over and over and the only time she'd looked up is if I pulled her back with my hand fisted in her soft curls and planted my lips firmly on her plump lips. The little nymph has said that I should feel free to interrupt her for breaks of that sort any time.

"I know you're hoping to get this guy and save Maddie from any of this but if my sources are reliable, and you know damn well that they always have been, I think you need to have her on alert. She is already telling Vi she thinks it's ridiculous she has to have someone accompany her to the grocery store and she is getting suspicious," Orion states. I know Maddie is getting frustrated with all the chaperones. She still thinks it's because of the other clubs and is now thinking I'm paranoid.

"Yeah, I know," I sigh, "Before I tell her, I want to know what you have found."

"Look, man, you've got to trust me. I think the best thing to do is get Guard, Ava, and Vi together with you two and get it all out at once. The girls will be able to provide support. I know Vi has figured out a huge part of this on her own. She knows shit is going down," he continues. "With everyone around, she will feel safer and know that we've all got her back."

"I trust you. I trust all of you. You want to set it up and come by in an hour?" I ask. I dropped my eyes to my boots, contemplating the possible reactions that might arise when Maddie hears all that's been going down.

"I'll get it together. And don't worry, bro, we do this, and nothing is going to get to her. She's part of our Pride pack. Nothing touches her," he states firmly. I know he's speaking from the heart. Orion never says shit he doesn't mean. He doesn't sugar-coat, and he doesn't falsify or embellish, he's a straight shooter. He plans, he executes. Steady as a rock, sometimes too steady and too cold. I know that shit wasn't always good for Orion. He has such a tight hold on his emotions that I wonder how he's able to let Vi into his life. I am happy that she has taken root in his life though; he deserves it. She has been chasing his demons away and doesn't even know it.

I slide the phone back into my pocket and make my way back to Maddie. She is sitting cross-legged on one end of the sofa, head down jotting down her notes, the other hand cradling her guitar. "Hey, Baby, you ready to take a break soon?"

Her head pops up looking a little bewildered. "What time is it? How long have I been at it?" Then she proceeds to apologize. "I'm so sorry, Honey. I lost all track of time."

I raise my hand to stop her. "I like hearing you and seeing you at work, Kitten." I walk over to her and slide in next to her, placing my arm over the back of the sofa, sifting my fingers through her thick soft hair. Maddie moves her work to the side. Her head tips back to meet my gaze. Her eyes and smile light up her face.

"Do you want to hear this new song I'm working on?" she beams.

"Absolutely."

Her fingers nimbly worked the strings, creating a sweet melody. She closes her eyes and begins to sway in time to the music and then the sultriest sound escapes those sweet lips. Completely intoxicating.

When do you know that you have it all? When does it all make sense?
It happens little by little, so slight but feels so right.
It started with a call, knocking through my thick defense.
It means so much to see the way you fight,
for me.
Sweet love, ohhhhh, sweet love, my heart was closed forever,
Until youuuuu. Until you.
You found me, you showed me that I can feel again.
Protect me, love me, hold me.

You will always come back for me.
You will always come back for me.

She stops slowly, like she's emerging from a sexy dream, her eyes flutter open, again looking up at me.

I am awestruck. This song is us.

I caress her cheekbone, feel her soft peachy skin, dip my head to taste the lips where the sweetest words were sung. I take her into my arms and nestle her close to me.

"That was beautiful, Baby," I say gruffly. My voice and heart are filled with emotions that I thought were long dead. "I will never leave you behind and if for whatever reason we are ever separated, I will come for you. This is us. Now and forever."

Her lips reach my chin. "I know."

"We have company on the way," I announce. "Vi, Orion, Ava and Guard are dropping by. You cool with that?"

"Sure. I love those guys." Maddie bubbles with excitement.

I hate that I have to drop this bomb on her. But the plan will be solid. She won't be left out there un-protected and dangling.

I'm laid out on the sofa with Maddie lying on top of me, her arms wedged between my chest and hers, her legs interlocking with mine, her face in the crook between my neck and shoulder. My one arm is locked around her waist the other is on her ass when the sound of the doorbell informs that our visitors have arrived.

Maddie starts to stir.

"Mmmm, I think they're here," she says as she rubs her temple against my chest.

"Yeah, Baby." I gently extricated myself from her warm supple body, lifting her to a sitting position. "I'll get the door."

"Kay," she mumbles, her sleepy voice still present.

I can hear voices outside the door. "What's taking them so long?" Ava asks innocently.

"Are you kidding me?" Vi responds in an incredulous tone. "What do you think they're doing Ava? Playing Monopoly maybe?", she taunts.

"You know, Vi, they could be watching a movie or something and maybe didn't hear the doorbell," she persists.

"Oh please," Vi declares.

I wrench the door open. "If it isn't Lucy and Ethel," I greet them. I lift my sight to Orion and Guard. "You two gonna let them take this act on the road?"

Guard bursts out laughing. Orion stifles the inclination to join him, while Ava and Vi looked up at me with laser eyes. Then Vi begins, "Well since I'm Lucy..."

"What? Who said you were Lucy?" Ava interjects.

Everyone stops when they hear roaring laughter from Maddie. Holding her stomach, bent over and laughing uncontrollably. The sight of her revelling in the pure enjoyment of my family is addictive and I start to chuckle, followed by the others.

Orion is the first to regain control. "Okay ladies, can we make it into the living room, so we can have our conversation *inside*?" He leads the way, grabbing Vi's hand, hauling her after him.

Maddie is sitting on the arm of the chair that Ava had claimed with Vi on the other side. I think it's best to do this quick, like ripping off a Band-Aid.

"Kitten, I need your attention. Guard, Orion, and the guys have been working with me to make sure that you're always safe. "

"War, let me, man," Orion interrupts. He gives me a pat on the shoulder.

"Maddie, we have been looking over some intel to make sure everything is clear with the rest of the MCs that attended the party where you performed. In doing this, we discovered there may be another threat. The MCs are cool. The fools that were loud and obnoxious were dealt with by their own clubs." Orion takes a few steps forward and plants his ass on the coffee table facing the women. "While we were doing surveillance, we discovered that there were some anomalies. When we moved you out of your apartment, we noticed that your garbage looked tampered with. When we started asking your neighbours, they confirmed a man had been hanging around the building. One of your neighbours even tried to confront him, but he took off. Then you mentioned that you haven't been able to find a photo album. All this made us take a closer look at the entire situation. Demon lifted a print from one of the moving boxes, confirming our findings."

He takes Maddie's hand and continues. "I researched. I hunted for answers and everything has led back to Jefferson Hendley." Maddie jerks her hand back. Her face is pale. She is frozen, paralyzed in fear. I stalked over to her and tug her into my lap, enveloping her in my arms.

"Baby, come back to me. Stay with me. Look at me, Kitten," I state firmly. She looks directly at me, "You are safe, Baby. And you are going to stay that way." She gulps and slowly nods.

"What else?", she asks, her voice barely audible.

I nod to Orion to continue.

"Maddie, he has been released from the hospital, but he has missed his counselling sessions so now the police are out looking for him. We are looking as well, and let's just say he better pray the cops find him first."

Guard stands over us. "You are family, Maddie. You are protected by all of us. My job as president is to see to that. We are solid and strong, we have this under control. We are keeping a close eye on you, Ava and Vi. We are asking that you help us by not taking chances and being diligent when you are out. You need to keep your eyes open and to let us know anytime you see even the slightest, most insignificant detail that's setting off your senses."

Maddie stands up and looks around the room at each of us. Then she speaks, "I can't stay here. I can't put Ava and Vi in danger. I can't let anything happen to any of you." She then turns to me, as tears stream down her cheeks, "I can't let anyone hurt you. I love you too much." She turns to get up from my lap and run to the bedroom, but I grasp her upper arm, binding her more tightly to me.

"Where do you think you're going, Kitten?" I turn her back to me.

"Anywhere where he can't find me, and you won't be in danger," Maddie returns.

"No," I tell her sharply.

"But..."

"NO," I confirm.

Orion stands with his arms crossed over his chest. "Maddie, there is no reason to run. We have a secure system in place and if he has been watching, he will already know about all of us. If Hendley is smart he will get the fuck out of town and run. If not, he will be facing off against Satan's Pride and he will not win."

Ava tried with great might to get out of the arm chair until finally with Vi's help, she got to her feet. "He's right, Maddie. Don't you dare think you have to leave. Firstly, we are not letting you go. Secondly, it makes no sense to go. Here we are in our territory, our home turf, where we can manage the situation. Out there, " she points to the window, "we are taking stupid chances. And I know that you are not stupid."

Vi has been silent up to this moment. She approaches quietly, takes Maddie's hand and leads her to stand by the fireplace, locking her arms arounds around her. "I know what he did to you. He needs to pay for that."

A confused Maddie asks, "How do you know?"

"I've done research of my own. This guy is desperate and desperate people make stupid mistakes. I know you're scared, and I know you think you're protecting us, but you're wrong. All you're doing is falling into his trap by running where you will have no defense. You need to trust us. You need to trust Satan's Pride," Vi says.

"It's a little insulting that you think that our MC can't protect you, Maddie," Guard adds.

Maddie's head turns sharply towards Guard. "I don't mean to insult you. He said he poisoned everyone I loved. What if he doesn't bluff this time?"

I've had enough, "Maddie, you are not leaving me. We made the decision to stick together and work it through. You can't tell me you love me and walk away. Come here, Baby." I wait for her to come to me then place my hands on either side of her face and stare into her eyes. " You belong to me and I belong to you." I kiss her softly. "No more talk about leaving, okay?"

Her hands clench my t-shirt at my hips and she takes a deep breath, "Okay. What's the plan, Honey?"

The next couple of hours pass quickly, talking about strategies and plans to have the Pride on alert and keep our women covered. Cris, Risk, and Demon join us to further discuss the current video system and how we can connect it to all the brothers' phones so that if backup is required the closest men can get there in less than a heartbeat.

Risk is almost done with the studio and needs to contract out for the installation of special recording equipment. He is currently doing background checks on each company and is demanding full disclosure on any employee that will be on the property.

As the afternoon unfolds, I can tell Maddie is more relaxed. Ava and Vi have rallied. I even hear them giggle. Sweetest sound in this mess of anguish.

Orion gives only the necessary information to girls to place them on alert. The rest of the fucked-up data he leaves for me and the Pride. They found a hotel he rented with a print-out of Maddie's lyrics covered in his semen. The thought of him jerking off to my girl sends me into a silent rage. I want to kill this fucker. There have been purchases of Ambien, a sleep drug, and small purchases from a hardware store for duct tape and other miscellaneous items on his credit card. Either he's stupid, or he's losing patience and is setting up for the take.

"War, brother," I hear from beside me. Risk places his hand on my shoulder. I pivot to face him.

"We got this, man. It's just a matter of time," he utters.

"Yeah," I confirm, "I just hate having her go through this again."

Guard pipes up, "She's stronger than you think. Her first thoughts were to save you, not herself. And this MC does not let fuckers take anything that doesn't belong to them. Maddie is yours, so now she is ours. She belongs to us. And no one touches what's ours."

"Play something for us. I love hearing you sing," Ava prompts.

"I'm not sure now is the time, Ava," Maddie replies. Her hand gestures towards us. "The guys are working things out. I don't want to distract them."

I take a step forward. "Baby, play our song again."

"Now?", she asks.

"Now is a great time. Play it again." My voice is low and meaningful. I don't have to say another word. She can tell how badly I want to hear those words of love and trust.

CHAPTER 17

You Say it Better

Maddie

To forget the turmoil of the afternoon, s War and I go to our first Friday night party at the club since the night I sang for them. I wasn't too sure this is wise but then War pointed out that this is exactly what we need. Friends and good food. It's only the Pride members and a few out of town charter members that have come in for a short stay. That still means that there are over fifty people at the compound having a blast. They are kicking back, enjoying the night. They congregate throughout the building, some playing cards, some just chatting and drinking in small groups. Others are dancing, swaying to the music. Some of the couples are dancing so seductively that I wonder if they're going to fully go at it right there on the floor. Thank goodness they curb their baser instincts.

War and I sit and chat with everyone and anyone who comes by. Risk sits and talks for a while and gives us further insights on the state of the studio. He has hand-picked the company that is coming on Monday to install the equipment. He is very friendly; however, I notice that he rarely speaks of himself. War discloses that he was a sniper in his past life. He is the hands-on guy, with an engineering degree and is an architect as well. From what I hear, he is brilliant. He is older than most of the brothers, though he's also super-hot. Not as hot as my man, but then again no one is as hot as War in my eyes.

I notice several glances between Orion, Risk, and Cris throughout the night. I am laughing with some of the girls who are often invited to their parties—Jessie, Tania and Lizzie. They are fans of The Smoking Guns and are excited to chat me up and ask questions. We are going to take selfies when Risk interrupted and relieves Jessie of her phone.

"No pictures," he states sternly before confiscating the phone. "You'll get it back at the end of the night."

I am about to pipe up when Vi leans into me and says, "Protection, Maddie. We don't want anything leaking your location for now." I get it. They are keeping me safe until they catch Jefferson.

I look over at the hot bunch of scary biker dudes, my hot guy being one of them, heads huddled in deep discussion. I hope all is well. They seem very intensely invested in their conversation. War snaps his head up, sensing I'm looking at him. This earns me a wink and a sly smile. I love that look on him.

It feels good to relax and be me. The ladies are sweet. When Ava waddles over, looking extremely swollen and tired, we all rushed to make her comfy on the couch, making sure her legs are elevated. She is coming up on her eighth month. I love that Guard greets her with such tenderness. His hand grazes her shoulder and gently cups her head then tips it back and kisses her softly. "Stay put, little mamma. You need anything, you ask someone to get it for you. You move from here and I put you back in the car and we head home," he growls against her ear, loud enough for us to hear. It's his way of requesting we treat Ava with care. I glance over to Vi and see a sadness lurking in her eyes. I want so desperately to chat with her alone, so I can help her through whatever it is that is bothering her, as she has been so strong and supportive of me throughout this entire situation. I follow her gaze and see she is staring at Orion, who is still immensely engrossed in his posse.

"Vi, you want to come over for lunch tomorrow?" I ask, hoping I'll be able to get her to open up to me.

"Sorry, Ava. I have to work tomorrow. I am also going over to Crossland County tomorrow, after work. I have some errands I need to run." Her eyes don't meet mine. I can clearly see that something is amiss.

I take her hand and squeeze, "I can come with."

"No, sweetie, it's just some silly errands," she shakes me off.

"Okay, but if you change your mind, I would be great company. We can sing to every silly song loud and off tune there and back," I hedge.

"Thanks, Maddie, but I really need some me-time." Just like Vi, tells it like it is.

"I know I haven't known you or Ava long, but I have grown to really love you two. Please know that I am here for anything you need." I embrace her.

"I know. And ditto." She looks back at Orion and says, "I'm going to go see if I can convince Orion to dance with me." Then she sashays over to him, swinging her hips with purpose. Orion instinctively wraps am arm around her waist as she nears, effectively ending our tete-a-tete.

War decides to stay the night in his room here at the compound. I only vaguely remember his space here since I was so exhausted that first night. I do remember waking in his arms, feeling safe for the first time in a very long time. I did remember how he looked at me on stage, like I was his rocker chick bad girl. I figured I'd surprise him with something a little naughty tonight. We extricate ourselves from the clan in the late hours of the evening, making our way to the privacy of his room.

As soon as we walk through the door, I'm backed up against it, one of his giant paws at my hip and the other beside my head. His lips are on mine and they're fierce and determined. I immediately respond, opening my mouth and dueling his tongue with mine. I almost forget my surprise but pull back and with a breathy voice said, "Honey, I need a moment in the bathroom. You won't be disappointed."

War's brows raise in an inquisitive look. He dips his head near my ear as I feel his lips leave a trail before saying, "Ok, Kitten, ten minutes, then I'm coming in after you." Those lips make my entire body quiver, half-ready to abandon the plan and have at him.

I slide out from between him and the wall, my breasts grazing his chest, my fingers gliding over his waist, lingering and trailing over the hard ridges of his abdomen.

I grab my overnight bag and head to the bathroom. I primped and preened earlier at home to make sure I'm silky soft and smooth. I quickly brush my teeth, then reapply a little light blush and lip gloss. I slide into a leather corset and matching black leather boy shorts that reveal a great deal of cheek. I fasten two leather arm bands enhanced with chrome designs that scream "Rocker Babe". The final piece of my "fuck me" outfit is a pair of patent leather heels with straps that wrap around my ankles, once again enhanced with more chrome notches and swirls.

Vixen Maddie is the opening attraction and sole performance in this show, starting with me opening the door and sliding only my leg out, ensure that my heel is featured. I hear a growl, which only encourages me to step out into the center stage of our bedroom. I strut out in full view of War reclining back to the headboard of the bed, shirtless, with a bountiful amount of tanned sexy skin showing. His jeans are unbuckled and loose and the V of his muscled body is evident. I take my fill of his beauty. I'm jolted out of my stupor when I hear, "God loves me, Baby. He gave me you."

I blink.

"Come here, Kitten, let me touch." War crooks his finger, motioning for me to move closer. I saunter over to the bottom of the bed, bending at the waist with both hands on the edge of the bed, giving him a full view of my breasts encased in the tight corset, cinching my waist and emphasizing my assets. I climb onto the bed and slowly, with intensified purpose, crawl between his legs. My lips lick, taste, and kiss the expanse of his exposed body. A hand wraps itself in my hair and drags my mouth to his in a sultry, deep kiss. I lose myself in his mouth. Tongues and lips. The tight grip holding me exactly where he needs to take his fill. When he finally breaks our connection, I'm completely breathless. My lungs gasp for air and I crave more of him.

"You may have had a plan for your seduction, Kitten, but I am taking over, yeah?" It's supposed to be a question but is most definitely a certainty. I nod, too breathless to think. I so very much love when he takes control.

He pulls me up to straddle his legs as he straightens, still resting back against the headboard. His hands slide from the straps at my ankles, with light circular motions, moving around my waist to my ass, cupping and massaging, slipping his fingers into the edge of my shorts until he reaches my clit and continues his sweet torture, circling his finger over my engorged clit. A moan escapes me. I grip his shoulders, throw my head back and arch my back to deepen the pressure.

"Eyes on me, Kitten," he orders. I right my head and meet the hot fire in his eyes. I move my body, grinding against his digits. "Get there, Baby. Fuck yourself on my fingers. I want you come all over my hand." His gruff voice brushes against my lips as his hand increases the pressure with two fingers dipping inside me while his thumb continues to stimulate my clit. I am panting against his lips and mewling for release. I rock hard against his hand. He increases his pace. He knows just what I need. My pussy clenches his fingers and I grip his hair, burying my head in his neck as I scream my release. His arm encircles my waist, holding me tight to him as he continues to cup my pussy.

"You're so beautiful. I love the sounds you make when you let go. The way you move on my body sets me on fire," his gruff voice careens in my ear as his hands roam over my body, pulling me back to indicate that he wants me to meet his eyes. "Ready for more?" he asks.

I nodded, not trusting my voice. I just came and I'm keen to have him inside me again. "Words, Baby."

I instinctively cup his jaw with my hand, kissing the corner of his mouth. "Yes, more." I say. He guides my hands from around his neck and places them behind my head.

"Link your hands together," he orders, "Don't move those hands until I say."

I lick my lips and stared into his face. His hands roamed over the corset. "I like the package, Baby, but I think it's time to unwrap my present," he murmured as he begins to unfasten the hooks holding the corset together. Every time he unravelled a hook, his lips take a little lick at the exposed flesh until I'm fully exposed, the corset tossed aside, War's fingers teasing my collarbone. His hands trace to the underswell of my breasts, making my nipples tingle and swell to form taunt peaks. His mouth closes over one and begins to suckle, generating a pool of wetness between my legs. My hands come undone and immediately War stops.

"Uh nah, keep those hands where I put them," he commands as he tweaks my nipples.

"I want to touch you," I say in a low voice.

"My turn, Baby. Stay still, let me have my turn," he growls before his mouth returns to the its mark, laving and suckling until I'm crying out and grinding my lower body on his protruding cock, still wrapped in his jeans.

I am tossed onto my back, legs thrown in the air against War's chest, slightly parted. "Still, Baby," he says. I wouldn't dare move. If he stops now, I think I'll die. Teeth mark my ass cheeks with little love bites as his hands slide the very short short-shorts, along my thighs, removing them inch by inch, savouring, licking and tasted the trail of skin exposed.

"Oh my God," I whisper. I moan deeply as his lips reach the back of my knees, the shorts now at my calves just above my fuck me heels.

He pulls my legs apart, as far as the shorts will stretch, bends my legs towards by chest. "Be my good girl now, Kitten. Don't move," War says with a sinister twist.

Right then, his mouth closes over my pussy, moaning as he slips his tongue inside me. "Ohhhhhh," I drawl out. I began to wriggle and am instantly bitten on my ass.

"No," is all he says. Then I feel a long, wet swipe from the back to the front of my pussy. My legs moved closer to my chest, so he can focus on tormenting my very swollen clit. I feel his fingers pump inside me fast and hard as his mouth concentrates on sucking my nub. I can barely recognize my own voice as I beg for release.

"Please, oh! Don't stop!"

"Such a good girl," I hear. "My sexy bad, good girl."

A hard thrust, long and deep, penetrates my pussy. His cock is hard and thick and merciless, and he continues to guide himself in and out over and over, in a steady pace.

"Faster," I beg.

"Take it, like I give it," he states as War persists in his steady fucking. He adds his finger to my clit and applies pressure until I am on the precipice of another orgasm.

"Oh, please, let me come." I beg.

That's when he pulls me close to him with my ass on his thighs as his cock hit me harder, deeper and faster. I lose my mind in a wrenching orgasm that lasts so long that I am barely getting my bearing when I hear the amazing sound of War's cry of release. His thick cock fills me with all he has. He rips my shorts off the rest of the way, spreading my legs wide and I watch as he pumps his cock in and out of me until it softens. His face shifts from deep concentration to euphoria, then kisses me deeply.

So perfect. I have never had anything as perfect as this moment.

He flips us so that he is on his back and I'm lying on his chest. I lift my chin and say with cheekiness, "Can I move my hands, yet?"

A second of silence before a loud chuckle envelops the room. He maneuvers so that we're eye to eye, his face beaming.

"Baby, you are it for me. You are soft and hard. Sweet and sexy. Smouldering and innocent. Trusting and smart. You are my everything. I love you, Maddie," he says these words and my throat closes with emotion. There are joyful tears in my eyes.

"I love you, too," I tell him. "You say it better, because when you say it, I believe you."

"Baby," he starts.

"No—you say it better. Let me have this," I reiterated as I lay my head on his chest and snuggle in deep.

"Okay, Kitten," I hear him say as I begin to drift off. I fall asleep wearing my sexy heels, though at some point in the night, War takes them off. I wake in the morning to find our legs intertwined. Perfect.

CHAPTER 18

Aim, Shoot!

War

I've met with my brothers for daily updates for the past three weeks. No sign of Jefferson, no further intel, until today. I set Maddie up at Millie's Diner to have some time with Vi. Ava has not been sleeping well at night and Guard has insisted that she spend more time at home, resting as much as possible. Risk is on watch as I connect with the rest of the guys for an update.

"We finally got another hit on his card," Orion announces.

We wait for him to continue.

"He rented a car yesterday. I located the car and tapped into the GPS function and have been tracking him. He went over two counties to Redmond. He hit up three spots. A pawn shop, an apartment complex, and an industrial area. Can't know for sure which places he actually hit in that area because he parked and probably walked the rest," Orion said.

"Where is this taking us?"

"Hold on, War. I have our charter club members in that area doing a search on where he hit and what he was after. I sent Demon to work alongside. He will call me as soon as he finds out more." He pauses, sighs and continues. "I had a man waiting at the car rental shop. He didn't show. The car was brought in by a nineteen-year-old kid. He said a man paid him fifty bucks to return the car."

"Shit!" I shout.

"Clearly, Jefferson is being cautious and knows that the cops are out looking. Desperate men make mistakes. We all know this. We are looking for the mistakes as we speak." Orion continues to tap the computer screen and pulls up some accounts. He points and continues, "This is him. He is running out of funds and he is desperate to start using cards. This makes him more traceable. It's only a matter of time, War."

"In the meantime, we just lost track of where he is right now, and we are spreading ourselves thin by sending Demon out of town, watching the women, and continuing to run the businesses. This makes us weak," I tell them, though I know they already know.

Guard bellows, "We are not weak. We have allies and we will call them in if need be." He's standing in his power stance, arms crossed, and legs solid, "Nothing touches this club without a fight. Nothing."

I can't shake this feeling. My gut is knotted like a twisted pretzel. "Something is going down, I can feel it."

"War…" Guard warns.

"No, you know me, Guard. My instincts are dead on. Something doesn't feel right. I know his plan is in motion. We know he was an amateur chemist. He's inventive, volatile, and crazy as a loon."

"We are getting the pieces together. In the meantime, we need a plan," Guard states. "Ava is covered. She is either with me or Moses."

Moses has the name of a leader, but his heart belongs to the Pride. He's a longstanding brother with brooding anger that simmers inside of him. His past is secret to everyone but Guard. I know Guard trusts him with Ava's life which means he is as solid as they come.

"Vi is with Orion or Priest," Guard continues. Orion nods his assent. Priest is our underground guy. Everyone talks to Priest. He is calm, calculated and resourceful. "That leaves Maddie. She is with you or Risk."

I nod.

"One last thing, our business does not suffer, the rest of you in this room do what you need to do to keep us standing strong," Guard finishes.

The brothers all agree.

I know they won't let me down, yet I needed to make sure I've covered my bases. I'm taking her to the shooting range.

"You want me to do what?" she asks later when we're at the counter at Sam's Shooting Range. I have several guns that I've collected and registered throughout the years. I have one with me at all times when I am out and have two hidden in the house.

I hold out my 38. It's small and light weight. It will be easier for her to handle. She is staring down at it, eyes wide open and mouth hanging to her chin in surprise.

"Kitten, take the gun," I tell her gently.

She is so cute, she looks up at me and then back down to the gun in my hands.

"I have never held a gun. This is not a good idea." She shakes her head, still staring at my hand.

I place the gun on the counter. Her eyes follow my hand. I tilt her chin up to me. "Kitten, I want to assure you that we have you covered in every way. This right here is for me. I want to make sure that if there was even the slightest opportunity that you should ever be found on your own, you will be protected. And, babe, this doesn't stop here. We are going to be spending an hour a day in my gym. I am going to teach you self-defence. This is about you having control of your own future and giving me peace of mind."

She sighs and turns her head to the gun sitting on the protruding shelf. Picking it up, she looks towards the target and points. She cocks her hip to one side, aims the gun straight out and gives a stern look, then she haphazardly flips her hair and turns back to me. "Always wanted to be Sabrina from Charlie's Angels. How do I look?" she asks.

I hug her from behind. "You're a natural, babe, but don't be anyone but you. I love you just as you are. Now let me show you how to hold the gun properly and get you practicing."

We spend the next two hours teaching her how to load, unload and shoot at the target. Maddie is a quick learner. She takes direction well. I am still holding her steady until she gets used to the kick back from the trigger.

"I want to try it by myself," she says.

I let go and step back. "Go for it, Kitten."

She points and shoots, hitting the edge of the paper, barley grazing the arm on the figure outlined on the sheet. I sense her frustration. "That's good," I tell her.

"No, it isn't. Don't patronize me, War," Maddie replied. Her head hangs low.

"Hey, listen. That was a great first try. Now you need to readjust your aim and try again."

She tried again, inching closer to the middle of the sheet.

"Again," I say.

She shoots once more. Closer still.

"One more time, Baby. Deep breath, focus. Aim, shoot!" I instruct in a firm voice.

The shot rings out and straight through the gut. She drops the gun onto the counter and jumps up and down like a child who just won a toy. She runs into my arms shrieking, "I did it. I did it!" She's smiling from ear to ear.

"Yeah, babe. You did it. We're coming back in a couple of days, so you can get even better." I hug her close.

CHAPTER 19

Stronger Inside and Outside

Maddie

The week is a series of trips to the range and working out in the home gym in War's basement. We've been lifting small weights to build my strength. The morning after my first workout with War, I could barely walk. Everything hurt. He exhausted me at night with lovemaking and tortured me with sparing and working out during the day. I am beginning to think he is a sadist.

War is relentless in his training. We spent time negotiating tactics to get out of holds and quick hits and jabs to shock the attacker into releasing for even a split second so that I can run for safety.

I'm in the kitchen making breakfast after yet another hour of working out, exhausted yet happy.

I smiled as I make the eggs and bacon, humming along with the radio. The song, "Walking on Sunshine" by Katrina and the Waves, is playing. I love this song. The smells of bacon sizzling in the frying pan fills the air.

War is taking a shower. I think I hear a crash and twist my body towards the sound. Did War fall?

"War?" I call out. Nothing. "War are you okay?" Still nothing. I stand silent. Why isn't he answering? I head towards our bedroom, then immediately come to a full stop. War's words come back to me, "If anything seems off, you make a call to Guard immediately, find an instrument you can use for a weapon if you're not close to the gun, and find a hiding spot. Avoid any face to face contact if at all possible."

I hear the creaking of the floorboards. I grab the heavy wooden cutting board that's within my reach along with my phone from the counter. I scroll to Guard's number and hit the button to connect. I hear a groan from the bedroom. As I hold the phone in one hand, I make my way towards it.

"Yeah, Maddie, that you?" I hear coming from the other end of the handset.

"Hurry! At the house, please hurry," I whisper loudly.

"On our way. Stay put, Maddie. Get somewhere safe and stay put," Guard reminds me.

"I think War is hurt. I need to go check on him." I say frantically.

"Maddie, you putting yourself in danger will not help War. He will never forgive himself if you put yourself in that position for him." Guard said gruffly into my ear, then he barks out orders to others.

"Please hurry, Guard. I can't see him, but I think something is happening to him," I plead.

"Hide; we're on our way," he says. I am moving toward the garage and am going to hide when I'm grabbed from behind. A hand over my mouth and one at my waist grabbing me and forcing me backwards. I drop the phone and board, clawing at the hand at my mouth.

Again, War's words come to me. "Baby, bite down hard anywhere you see flesh. Elbow in the face, aim for the nose. Then run for help."

I fight. I bite, elbow, punch, and kick until I'm dropped. I scream for War and start to run. Right into War's arms. I bury myself in his arms crying. He holds me close, a hand at my head while murmuring sweet words to calm me down.

"Shh, you're okay, Kitten. Calm down," he says, quieting his voice.

I am shrieking, "He's in the house we have to go." I pull at his arms, trying to drag him out with me.

"Maddie, calm down. It's me, Risk." I hear behind me.

I turn to face Risk. What the hell?! He damn-well scared the hell out of me. I was shaking both from shock and fury. I turn and stomp to Risk and just as I'm about to give him a piece of my mind, I'm pulled back by War. I'm about to tell him to let go when I notice he doesn't have a scratch on him. What was that moaning and creaking? Where was the crash coming from? I look back and forth from Risk to War.

"What's going on?" I ask suspiciously.

"Sit down, Maddie." War said.

I sit and wait. "You're going to get upset. But I want you to know that I arranged for Risk and me to setup a possible abduction, to see how you would react," he says matter of factly.

"You did what?" I ask, confused. Then my fury erupts. I stand and go nose to nose with War, which isn't easy because I have to stand on the sofa to do this. "Do you have any idea how terrified I was? Did you think this is funny? I thought you were hurt or worse and I couldn't reach you. I was panicked and scared. I called Guard who is on his way over here right now with a crew of your brothers, who, when they get here, I hope kick your asses for putting me through this." I have my hands on my hips and I'm yelling at an octave that would make anyone's ears bleed. My chest is heaving. I am fuming mad when I turn to Risk, "And you, I thought we were friends. I made you a Maddie pie and I don't just make those for anyone. Ask Demon, he knows. He's been letting me know he wants a pie by leaving me notes, because he won't actually say more than one word at a time, and I didn't make him another pie." I am now ranting and blubbering and even to myself I know that I am making little to no sense at all.

War grabs me and tries to force me onto his lap. I struggle, wriggling to get back up. "Kitten, settle down," he commands. "Listen to me. Then if you want to continue being mad, you can be mad."

I fold my arms across my chest and sit stiffly on his lap, because he won't allow me to move. "This I have to hear. Go ahead, wow me," I say sarcastically.

"Watch that sass, Baby, or I will have to spank that ass," War says with a smirk and twist of his lips. Then his voice gentles as one large gentle hand cups my cheek, as his thumb moves over my lips. "Babe, I have been working with you for a while. Risk and I are aware that elements beyond our control can happen no matter how much we plan. I wanted to make sure that you would be able to get safe if I wasn't able to get to you. You and my family here are the most important people in my life. I would gladly die for you to ensure your freedom and happiness. Today was to prove to you that you are strong enough to fight back and win. I hated doing this to you. I hated to see the fear in your eyes for even a moment. Today you fought back, and you fought hard. I think you gave Risk a bruise or two."

I think on his words. He wants me to see my own strength. He wants me to fight back, to remember the plan we put together. I am still hopping mad. I understand his premise, but I don't like how he went about it.

"He deserves those bruises," I tell him grimly. I look over at Risk; he rubs his jaw and stares back. His glare is better than mine. "You have a lot of explaining to do when Guard gets here," I add smugly.

"Kitten don't get pissed. He's not coming. He knew what we were doing. If we were in imminent trouble, we have men on parole around the property. You will always be safe."

"Everyone knew but me?" I'm extremely hurt. Did Ava and Vi know what they had planned? Wouldn't that be a breach in our girlfriend code?

"Ava and Vi had nothing to do with this." War says, reading my mind. "Please, Kitten, I know this is upsetting now but understand that this was not only for my peace of mind but for you to see how much *you* can accomplish."

I am not letting him off the hook that easy. "You terrified me." I tell him. "I need to think on this. You need to let me up, so I can do that."

War releases me and lets me up. I walk to the kitchen and without glancing back, I say, "When breakfast is ready, you and Risk are going to come and eat. Neither of you are going to complain that the bacon is burnt because that's your fault. Or the toast. Again, your fault."

"Yeah. Kitten, no complaints." I hear him say.

As I'm working in the kitchen, I think about everything War has said. It was a crumby thing to do, regardless of the meaning behind the operation. I replay the events in my head over again. I stayed true to plan for the most part. There was room for improvement, but I held my own and was able to get out of a bear-like hold by Risk, who is one massive hulk of a man. I smile at the grunt of pain I evoked from Risk when I snapped my elbow back into him. I call the guys to the table for breakfast.

"Before we start, I want to say that I don't agree with your method, however, I will admit that today did confirm that our training is working. I know I am getting stronger inside and out. Yes, I panicked and lost sight of that for a moment but I bounced back quickly."

War reaches over, tugging my hand until our lips meet. "You *are* stronger, inside and out, Baby. I'm proud of you."

And that was that, I was back to calm and War had peace of mind.

CHAPTER 20

You've Got to Trust Me with Your Life and Hers

Orion

Finally, the pieces of the puzzle are beginning to fit together. The information is making sense. Sick, demented sense. Jefferson Hedley is a sick son-of-a -bitch. Each piece of intel delivered from Demon, Ghost, and Cris, together with the internet hacking, disclosed the demented thoughts of a mentally deranged man.

I have reviewed the details over and over. I know that I must gather our Pride brothers and get to him before he has the opportunity to get to Maddie. War is going to lose his fucking mind, which is a critical problem. A hot temper leads to mistakes. Mistakes in this case may lead to a fatality. Jefferson is not afraid of dying and taking Maddie with him. This is a goddamn mess!

I throw my hand down on the desk, the vibration jarring the entire contents covering the surface.

"Hey, babe, is everything okay?" I hear Vi's voice at the door. She raps lightly against the door, once more. "Orion?"

"Vi, I need you to find something to do," I say harshly. I know that I am being unfeeling, however, this is not the issue I want her to be involved in. She is too smart for her own good. She gets an inkling that she can help and save her friend, Maddie, she will be all over it. I will lose my shit if she puts herself in danger. Vi jumps into action with no regard for herself.

I have let Vi into my life more than I ever expected. I even let her stay the night, even the weekend. I haven't allowed a woman to be more than a casual fuck since I lost my wife, Christine.

Vi's faint voice from the other side of the door seeps through, "I'm going home. Don't bother coming to see me out." The click clacks of her heels resonate through the hall.

No fucking way, Vi is leaving this house without protection. I grab all the paperwork I need and rush to head her off at the front door.

"Yo, Vi, don't move." I see her hand on the door knob.

"I can see myself home," she said with looking back.

"I take you home, sweet thing," I lower my voice, reaching out to stroke her hair. She still doesn't move. I brush my lips to the top of her head.

"Sure," she whispered.

I texted Guard to tell him we needed to meet and that I need Priest to watch Vi. We drive in silence. Vi has become quieter lately. It worries me but, in this moment, I need to concentrate on the matter at hand; I will address this after we deal with Maddie's stalker.

I walk her to her small apartment above Millie's Diner. She kisses me lightly and turns to walk away. I pull her back and kiss her soundly on the mouth. She melts into me immediately. My Vi, a ball of fire, yet sweet like a candy. "I will call you tomorrow," I told her.

I head to our meeting spot. We meet at Reggie's bar, just outside of town. It's one of our establishments. It's a bar and this is where the guys come to unwind. Guard is rarely here anymore since Ava come along. He knows how crucial this is and is pulling up into the drive. The roar of his pipes gets louder until he pulls in.

"Hey", I greeted him with a chin lift. Guard mimics my motion.

"We'll talk in the office," Guard said.

We arrive to the inner circle of our crew, less one, War. I wanted to get everyone on board with the plan I devised before we spring it on War. He's going to hate it. We either force Jefferson's hand or we risk having the girls on lock down for an undetermined amount of time. I already know that Guard is beginning to lose patience. His baby is arriving and that is one more concern.

After having gotten everyone's attention, I laid it out.

"Here is what we are dealing we, Jefferson has an apartment that he is renting under an assumed name, Jeff Morris. We confirmed this by showing his picture around the building and neighbourhood. His neighbours think he is a great guy and always willing to help out. He is moving his fiancée in very soon. His fiancée Maddie is a musician and she is on tour. He is proposing when she is back in town. This is how he explains his absence; he is visiting her on tour while setting up their love nest," I paused for a second to let this all sink in.

Guard prompted, "Go on."

I sigh before I give them the rest, "Jefferson went to a set of factories and labs, on the pretence that he was meeting a realtor to rent space. I have a feeling that something was weird in him choosing a lab, so I hacked into their system and found a shitload of emails about some missing chemicals and gases. This was not two days after his visit. They reported the missing shit to the cops and they are looking for him as a suspect. Cops haven't been able to pick up his trail."

I point to Risk and Demon. "Our two brothers have found that before Maddie, this shithead had his site on another woman. In a span of a few months, her boyfriend left her leaving only a note, she was constantly receiving surprise visits from him and when she refused him, he lost his shit. He took her from the parking lot where she worked. She was smart enough to tell her boss what was happening and when she screamed bloody murder, he called the cops and got the plates of his van that he threw her into. They found her a few hours later, beaten to near death, with a note from the fucker. The note read, "You are redeemed. I have beaten the demon out of you. Rest in peace."

"Fuck me," Guard spit out. The tense fury reverberated around the room.

"The woman, Lisa, survived. And after a year of rehabilitation she was physically recovered. Her family moved her home and it took two more years before her life returned to somewhat normal." I stopped for a minute and pulled out my plan. "This plan is rough, but it will smoke him out. War will lose his shit. I wanted to get your take before we move on this," I finished.

We reviewed the plan for hours, to each minute detail to ensure the safety of Maddie and all our Pride. We also anticipated every question and conflict that War was going to engage.

Risk was unusually quiet until he said, "What if we don't give him all of it? What if we give him what he needs to know so that sees the minimal risk to Maddie?"

"We don't play that way," Guard replied.

"You know that a conflicted man with a personal interest works on emotion. I admit that War has always been cool and strategic but now there is Maddie."

"Tell me that you have your sister or mother in this situation, you wouldn't want to know it all?" I questioned.

"Point made," Risk responded.

"Call him, Orion," Guard commanded.

The conversation was brief. We sent a sentry to watch over Maddie while we waited for his arrival and went over the plan once more.

War stalked into the room and knew immediately that something was up. He stood in the middle of the room surrounded by the Pride. I approached. One hand on his shoulder, the other over my heart, "You have to trust me with your life and hers. I swear vengeance for what he put her through, we all do. War do you trust us."

"With my life," he said without hesitation. A second later, "And hers."

We surrounded the table. Mission "Free Maddie" was on.

CHAPTER 21

I Take My Life Back

Maddie

War left in a hurry. It's not often War runs out and I've discovered that if he is on the move to meet the club then it must be over something important. I've always had Paul to lean on. I know that he feels responsible for not being able to stop what happened to me and that has played a part in our relationship. I know when he is back from tour and sees the strong me I used to be before the pain, we'll be able to be more playful with each other again. I look forward to him coming home.

I decide to head to bed knowing I have protection circling the house. I'm wiped. I had the great idea of wanting to throw a baby shower for Ava. I want to thank her for her encouragement and support, for reminding me that I can laugh, for sharing her best friend, Vi, and for embracing me into her life and introducing me to a new set of gal pals. When I mentioned this to Vi, she thought it was a fabulous idea. Since she is so creative and talented, she is doing the decorations. We decided on a simple BBQ with a baby theme. Baby burgers (or mini sliders), baby sized hotdogs (let me tell you how hard they were to find), mini sized fries, mini cheesecakes personalized for each lady we are inviting, and a big beautiful cake that says baby boy with a mini Harley. Vi told me to prepare because they guys will crash the party and there had better be super-sized versions of everything as well. So that's on the menu, too. All Ava has been craving is burgers and hot dogs and I decide that fancy isn't necessary but being true and real is.

I'm in a state of half-sleep when I hear War come into our bedroom. The rustle of his clothes faintly drifts through the air as he undresses. The bed descends as the weight of his body hits the mattress. His arm curves over my waist dragging me from my side of the bed to the centre, his fingers holding me tighter than normal. War's body is tense. It's clear that whatever happened at their meeting tonight has upset him.

I turn to face him. Oh yes, something is definitely wrong. His jaw is stern, his eyes narrow, his brow furrowed, beaconed by the moonlight. He is clearly disturbed. I wrap my arms around his middle, forcing him onto his back so that I am semi-laying on top of him.

"Honey are you all right?" I ask.

His fingers grip my waist a little, "No," he says, his voice gruff and curt. No bullshit. No hiding his sentiments.

"Do you want to talk about it?" I try again.

"Not tonight," War's low voice hums as he kisses the top of my head.

Well, clearly talking is not the answer to lessening the tension. I have never been very good at instigating sex. I've been more adventurous with War as the days and weeks have passed, although I'm yet to completely rid myself of my shyness and I'm not sure I ever will. Throwing caution to the wind, I slide my hand across his hard chest to his circle is nipple. I place soft butterfly kisses over his chest, guiding my myself further onto his body. I kiss and lick all the way to his mouth. His hand fists gently in my hair, cradling my head in his grip.

My lips are poised above his, our breaths mingling. "I love you, War Xander Cole, with all that I am and all that I will ever be. Each moment with you is so precious. You made me see my strength, my talent, and the beauty of what we have."

I notice War's eyes glisten with unshed tears. His voice hard with emotion, "You had all that before me. I was just fortunate enough that you blessed me to be the man you share it with."

And just like that, my own eyes fill with tears. Although, unlike War, I cannot stop them from falling to my cheeks. He wipes one away with his forefinger and another with his lips grazing my face. His whiskers brush my face. I adore the scruffiness of his whiskers against my skin. His body is hard and firm against mine.

"Tonight, Maddie, I want to make love to you. I want to cherish every part of you," he whispers huskily against my lips.

"Oh, yes." I murmur as he guides me further into him with a scorching, long, sensual kiss that makes my body come alive. I vibrate from head to toe. He turns us so that I'm underneath his body and he proceeded to cherish each and every part of me. His lips move across my face in soft kisses, moving back to my mouth in yet another deliciously agonizing kiss that sets my body on fire. I slide my hand up his back, feeling every bit of him. He continues to brand my lips with his touch. He goes from licking and teasing to sucking them gently, lolling them about in his mouth, making me grow wetter and wetter between my legs. I squirmed beneath him, opening my legs so that his are firmly set between mine. War takes no notice and continued his ministrations. His mouth makes its way down my body and hovers over my sex, as his fingers pull and gently twisted my nipples. I lift my hips, careening to move closer to his mouth. He gives me what I needed. I gasp as his wet silky tongue ravishes my pussy. There is no part of me he hasn't kissed, licked, nipped, or sucked. I'm on the very brink of ecstasy, back bowed off the bed, head back against the pillows, eyes slammed shut waiting for the touch that will send me over the cliff.

"Maddie, look at me, Baby. See me come inside you." War's sexy rough voice forces my eyes open. "Watch us, Baby. Watch me come," he repeats.

With what feels like super human strength I raised myself on my elbows and stare down to see his huge, beautiful cock slide inside me inch by inch. He strokes himself deep inside me growling, "My Maddie, my woman, my love." As he pulls out and thrusts deep again and again, over and over, he says, "Forever mine. It will always be you for me, Maddie."

His cock juts in and out at a slow pace and it isn't enough; I needed more. "Faster, Honey."

"I want to take it slow, Kitten, I like to see myself move inside you."

Oh my God, I can't take it. I wrapped my legs tighter around his hips. Just then his finger slides to my clit, placing just the amount of pressure to send me over the edge. I scream his name over and over, my pussy clutching his cock, my hands imprinted in his arms. I can hardly catch my breath when I am turned over onto my hands and knees and feel his hardness enter me again, hard and fast, building me up to yet another orgasm. His fingers pinch my nipples, his legs splay mine further apart so that I have only my forearms on the bed to balance as he continues to plunder inside me. I am so sensitive to his touch that when his body cloaks over mine and whispers, "Come for me again, Baby. Now," my body answers his demand immediately, followed by his roar of release. We both lay exhausted on the bed, embraced in one another's arms.

"I love you, Maddie. You are my one." The most beautiful words I've ever heard as we both drift off to sleep. Although I know this temporary intermission did not take away the problem that War is currently dealing with, I do know that for a brief time, it was only him and I. Tomorrow will come. War will share what and how he needs to, and I will be here to see it through alongside my man.

I blink slowly to the sun dawning into the room. Again and again, until all comes into focus. That all is glorious. My hand drapes over a luscious bare chest, rising and dropping with each deep breath. My eyes saunter to the full length of his tapered V, rippled with muscle, hip and legs covered with a white sheet, like this was a design ad for bedding and with this image every woman would be running to buy out the stores if it would bring a man like War to their bed. I tilt my head back to take in the rest of him. No one would ever say he looked delicate, even in his sleep, he does however look peaceful. I noted that throughout the time we've been connected, he rarely looked peaceful. War is thought-filled, guarded, and positioned to strike almost always. I like to think that I'm giving him peace in my arms.

I slide my arm off his chest, noting that he hasn't moved a muscle. He must be drained. I slip from the bed and instigate my morning ritual. I wash up quickly and decide that breakfast in bed would be a nice surprise. And after having donned some baby blue yoga pants and a stretchy matching tank top, I march into the kitchen to whip up some French toast.

My mom made the best French toast. It's one of the few great memories I have of my youth. I loved it so much I always knew that as an adult, I would make it for special occasions and for people I truly cared for. So far that list had been Paul and our crew. They are my family. Today I make it for War. I finish putting the caramelized apple over top and set it on a tray I found tucked behind a cupboard, alongside coffee and juice before prancing back to the bedroom. I hear the shower being turned off as I approach the door and my eyes get their own special treat as I see War wrapped in nothing but a towel covering his man bits. A very small towel at that. I remember that I forgot to replace his towel. Can I say how happy I am that I neglected to take a spare towel from the closet before my shower?

"Babe, you keep staring at me like that we're not going to leave this room for the day and we have plenty to do today," he sends a smirk my way.

I snap out of my trance, raise the tray and say, "I thought I would treat you to breakfast in bed." I place the tray on the bed. War grabs a pair of boxers from the dresser, quickly gets dressed and comes over to the bed.

"Kitten, that looks amazing. No one has ever made me breakfast in bed," he informs me.

"You're up now. Would you rather have it in the kitchen?"

"No way. My girl makes me a surprise breakfast, I am going to enjoy every second of it. In bed." He makes his way back to the bed, pillows propped behind him. "Bring it over, Baby. Sit beside me."

I placed the tray over his thick thighs. "I have a plate in the kitchen for me." I scurry to the kitchen and back with my plate, making my way in beside him.

I watch him take his first bite, his eyes open wide, and a moan escapes his lips. "This is the best thing I have ever tasted. Baby, you have made me some wonderful meals, but this tops anything you have ever made." His hand reaches the back of my head and he draws me close, kissing me lightly on the lips.

Risk and War are supervising the installation of the equipment in the studio today. Risk promises it will be completed today. He is going to give me a tour and explain all the security features. I wanted to go now but they said I would slow down the process and completion of the project.

And speaking of things moving along, Vi and I have been making progress on our plans for Ava's baby shower. We rented a tent and the guys agreed to BBQ. We ordered a specially designed cake with a mini leather jacket and booties design. I can't wait to see what else the baker might incorporate in the cake. She is a genius and thankfully lives right here in our own backyard. She runs a small kitchen, only taking orders without the space to display her artful desserts. She supplies Millie's diner with all her baked goods and is the go-to for special occasions and events in town. Thank goodness Vi works at Millie's and knew about her sinful delights! Everything is planned and set for next Saturday afternoon. All the girlfriends from the Satan's Pride crew have been invited as well as some close friends that Vi has made in town. I am looking forward to surprising Ava. Guard is on board and since he was so worried about her being on her feet, we had a plush pink over-stuffed leather chair purchased and set to be delivered the morning of the party.

I am deep in the middle of my gift for Ava and baby biker boy when Risk saunters into the room. I swear this crew of men have cornered the market on gorgeous and it's no wonder the female population hang around like groupies waiting to get noticed.

"Hey." I smile at Risk.

"Maddie." He acknowledges my smile and adds a teasing curve to his lips.

"Can I get you guys anything? You've been out there for hours."

"We're done. I came in to take you out and show you what we've put together. You can fill me in if anything is missing or if you want anything else added," he states.

I jump off the couch and run to the door, passing Risk and chattering, "Let's go! I've been dying to see it." I can hear the rumble of chuckling as he follows me out the door.

I step into my studio and am awestruck at the detail and care that has been given to this project. It's amazing. It had the latest equipment and I know it's the best because I researched this over and over, wishing I had my own space and thinking that one day I might have this for myself. I touch the buttons on the console and look around. My CDs and awards are framed and mounted on the walls. War has even taken the time to look through my pictures and hand-picked some great shots of me and Paul, the entire band, and one of me singing. The one of just me is from the night of the concert with Satan's Pride. I was so deep into the song that every emotion is visible on my face.

Risk interrupts my thoughts. "Let me show you the security I installed." I shake my head a little to refocus my attention on Risk.

"Here is the key pad. Code is 623343. You walk in and immediately the code needs to be entered. Once you are in you will re-enter the code to rearm. When you leave you will have twenty seconds to enter the code to arm it before locking the door. It is rigged that the lock must trigger in order for the alarm to be secure and will send a signal if it is not," he states. He shifts his attention to the space throughout the room.

"I have made special provisions for this room that no one knows about, Maddie. Not even War. I did the work myself and I know it's solid." His voice is serious, and his gaze states the same.

He walks across the room to the wall. The wall is wainscoted in a cream colour with antique accents throughout. A row of buttons is on the wall. He goes through each one, pointing at each as he explains their importance. "This one work the microphone on/off, this moves it across the ceiling and back, this one locks it in place." He waves me over to come closer. I approach and he points to the last button. "This one is for emergency use. This button," he hits the button and a panel slides open in the wall, "is for a panic room."

I know my mouth is open. I gape at the space in the wall. Then look up at Risk. Then back to the room. "Oh my God," I whisper loudly.

Risk ignores me and continues. "This room is if you hear anything happening outside or if someone is trying to get in here that you believe is a danger. It only fits three and that's a tight fit. If anyone is trying to get in here, chances are they want you or Paul. You two get in here and the others leave through the emergency exit in the back." He points to a door that I thought was a closet and understand he hasn't labelled it so that it won't tip anyone off.

But Risk isn't done. "In this room there is an emergency phone. It connects directly to the club and there is always someone who will pick up. It goes through every phone of every member and someone will pick up. I have placed some water and protein bars as well as blankets in there just in case we have to act cautiously and may take some time to get you out. Chances are you will never need to use them, but I would rather have them there than not. This room is impenetrable however if someone by any dumb luck finds a way in, I have a gun placed here." He walks me into the room and on the built-in shelves I see the blankets and other items he mentioned. Risk reaches for the black case and in it is the same model gun that I have been practicing with at the shooting range, ammo included.

His hand touches my arm and I look up at him. "You mean everything to him. Now you mean something to all of us. We are keeping you safe. Not only from this lunatic but however and whenever you need to be safe."

I mean everything to him. He means War. War has publicly declared this to his brothers. I blink up at Risk. "I'm taking my life back," I said.

Risk looks at me curiously, "What?"

"He has taken enough time out of my life. I am taking my life back." I look at Risk. "I hate that War is constantly having to worry about me. I hate that I have caused you all distress. That stops today. He doesn't get anymore." I state.

"Maddie, you are not to do anything foolish," he starts, but I interrupt him.

"No never. I would never do anything to cause you guys any more grief. I want him caught. I want this to end so Ava and Vi can lead normal lives. I want to see War settled so that we can go on our ride together and laugh freely."

"We have a plan," he says.

"What is it? How can I help?" I ask.

"War is waiting in the house. That's our next stop," Risk smiles.

Risk makes me practice opening the panic room and loading and unloading the gun and then teaches me how to make sure it is sealed properly when we go inside, just in case we ever have to use it.

CHAPTER 22

Colour of the Sky

Maddie

War is on his cellphone. His side of the conversation is limited to essential words only. The occasional "Yea, brother", "Got it", "Stay with him", and the one that he emphasizes the most is, "All eyes". He is so concentrated on the call that he is unaware Risk and I are in the room. He stands by the large window, looking out onto our property, his forehead leaning against the pane of the glass. He is anguished with worry. He is worried about me and his brothers. I am not sure who was on the other end of the phone however I know that he was reassuring War and with a heavy sigh and a final, "Thanks man", it's the end of the call.

Risk decides to announce our presence. "Yo, we're back."

War turns to face us. I stride over to meet him. I roll to my tiptoes and brush my lips against his. His fingers squeeze lightly at my waist. I love that. I also love that crinkle in his brow when I surprise him. I plan on surprising him more often.

War does his chin lift to Risk. It must be in the hot biker playbook.

"Take a seat, Kitten. I want to run something past you," War says. I curl into the corner of the couch. It's become my spot and one of my favourite places to write.

"War, I want you to stop thinking I am going to fall apart. I am strong; you let me see just how strong I am." I tell him.

"I'll start by telling you that we are not alone in this. Orion has devised a plan. It's good. It's solid," he states.

"But…?" I fill in the hesitation.

"We know he's out there and we know he has eyes on us. Not just you, but us. He knows the club has you under protection and he is hiding in the shadows, waiting for an opportunity for us to make a mistake," War spits out. His voice is rough, I can see that he hates being in the defensive state we are in.

"The plan is to let him think we are vulnerable and to let him make his move. We have all areas covered. You will be watched at all times however we are try-ing to make it look like he may have a shot at getting close," Risk pipes up.

"Right," I replied with a shaky breath. War takes my hand.

"We can throw away the plan and just wait for him to get tired of waiting and make his move. We don't have to do this. If you aren't comfortable, we stop this right now."

"No. I want this done. I am not living in fear. I am not letting him rule our lives anymore," I look at his concerned eyes and frame his face with my hands. "I trust you, War. And I trust Orion and Risk and Guard and all the other guys. I am all in and I am ready."

He closes his eyes briefly. As he opens them, he covers my hands with his. "You humble me, my beautiful woman. You are resilient, talented and I love you. I will not lose you," he states firmly.

"You will not lose me," I confirm.

"Right so let's get this plan moving," Risk interjects. He launches into the plan of attack. He unfolds the idea of a diversion and having to send some of the guys to assist another club, thereby making us appear vulnerable. The idea is to let him know that we will be relying on the alarm system in the house to alert us and since he believes himself to know all there is about technical equipment and computers…

According to all the research done by Orion and his crew, they believe he will take full advantage as soon as opportunity is presented. Ava's shower is coming up on Saturday and if this plays out as expected, this will be done and over by then.

I know where all the guys are going to be, and I know that although I may not see them, they will be around. The hardest part is knowing that War needs to be away for short periods of time to show vulnerability. He hates this more than I do and has been very vocal about it. Orion is right though, this will be over if force the situation. Burner phones are going to be used for real discussions and our regular phones to for generic conversation. Based on Orion's finding,

Jefferson has purchased, on credit, hacking equipment and we are going to lead him to us. Buying on credit means that he is running out of money. Desperate times equals mistakes. This was a mistake and Orion is homing in on him.

Tonight, the guys are having a "meeting", in other words laying the ground work that they will have to send some of the guys out of town. I am reminded once again that I have a weapon in the house and I have the ability to get free of different holds and run. The Satan's Pride brothers will be in a meeting with a selected few hiding in the shadows. Chances are that he will not strike tonight, but if he does, I will not go down without a fight.

I spend the night with my guitar. I want to give Ava, Guard, and baby a special gift. The love between Ava and Guard created an incredible extension of themselves filled with the greatness of each parent. What better way to celebrate and encase this special life than with a song made and dedicated to this family? I tease Ava that they should call their little man Avgar. Part Ava, part Guard. I embrace the emotions that I feel when I hear them talk, touch, kiss and even when they do nothing but sit in each other's company, laughing with the close group of family they have created for themselves. The lyrics start to flow and "Color of the Sky" comes to life.

What would I do without you?
Now that I see you here.
My world would be bland without you,
The colours all disappear.

The red is the joy you bring me,
The blue is true and real.
The green is hope of future,
The yellow shines through the rain,
The colour of the sky is you and all that you bring.

What would I do without you?
Now that I see you here.
My world would be bland without you,
The colours all disappear.

Your father's eyes I pray for
Your mother's smile I see,
Your loving heart within you,
Severing all our fears.
The colour of the sky is you and all you bring.

What would I do without you?
Now that I see you here.
My world would be bland without you,
The colours all disappear.

I sit and sing it over and over until I feel I have just the right words to express the family they've created. I like it now I hope they like it too. I want to record it on a CD. I'll sing it for them at the baby shower, but I know that a copy for them that they can play for baby will mean a lot. Tomorrow I will use my recording equipment for the first time. I find this so exciting. I have always wanted my own recording space that I can use whenever the mood strikes, and War has made my dream a reality. My warrior, my dream man.

War calls on the burner phone to let me know that he is on his way home. I usually wait for him to come in before heading to bed and am following suit when he tells me to head into bed. "Baby, we are bringing the message that we are comfortable and that he is no longer a threat. This means we need to change our patterns. Get ready for bed. I will be there soon. You okay with that, Kitten?"

"I got this," I tell him firmly. I do have this. I am not the weak-minded teenager he threatened years ago. "See you soon, Honey."

I get ready for bed. Sleep is elusive. I'm not afraid; I'm missing my man. As I begin to settle into sleep, I feel his body climb in behind me, wrapping me up in his arms. I revel in the warmth and nod off almost immediately.

CHAPTER 23

Never Again

War

It's been three days since our plan was brought into play. We had texts out to five brothers, letting them know they are riding out to assist our sister club close by. They ride out and circle around the state on silent watch. Each man is strategically placed, monitoring the house, studio, and property.

To play it right, we have never sent Maddie out alone. That would have been too obvious, and Jefferson would know that I would never let her be on her own. Our younger members, prospects, have been assigned Maddie. The men are more than qualified to look after my girl. Jefferson is going to get a huge shock when he makes his move. The men are ready; I am ready. Maddie has every right to be nervous. I am astounded by her resilience and strength. She is just going through her day. I can see her being cautious, yet she goes about town, meeting with Vi about the party for Ava, having coffee at Millie's, going to the club or just hanging out at home or in her studio.

Today she is hanging in the studio. She gushed about it to her brother over the phone the other night. Paul was just as enthused, and they started to plan a schedule for his return with the rest of The Smoking Guns to hit the studio and start recording again.

My burner goes off. "Hey," I answer.

Orion's gruff voice bellows through the phone. "He's making his move man. He is sitting on the edge of your property. We've got to wait for him to make a more solid move to take him down. Everything we have on him was gathered outside the boundaries of the law. We want more than a slap on the wrist. We want him to be put away for a long while."

"I'm on my way."

"We have a plan, remember. You do not get close yet," Orion says.

"Yeah, I know. I know." I slam my phone shut, mount my bike, and head to the lake on the edge of the property.

Maddie

I have my headphones on, listening to the recording I put together for Ava and Guard. I am pleased with the sound. The melody is light and happy. Vi is on her way over with a picture of Ava and Guard from one of their barbeques. We are going to imprint the picture on the CD and the cover. I already wrote the card, congratulating them on their baby boy's arrival. I add a personal note. I wanted them to know how thankful I am for creating the circumstances that brought me to War.

War has been on edge since they instigated their plan to smoke out Jefferson. I haven't seen him anywhere. I act as natural as I can, knowing that he is out there. Orion wasn't wrong in taking the offensive in this situation. The waiting is the worst. Realistically I know that full measures have been taken to secure my safety, emotionally I feel that he is lurking close and I must be prepared for anything.

I sense that something is amiss. I take off the headphones. I feel the door to the studio rattle. No one has knocked. No one but Vi is expected and she would be screaming down the house for me to open up or she would call my cell to tell me she is here. The guys would be calling me on the burner phone or would be knocking until they were heard. This is wrong. This feels wrong.

I grab my cell and make my way to the panic room. I hit the button and slide inside, securing it shut just as I hear the front door of the studio slam against the wall.

"Where are you hiding, sweet Maddie?" I hear that voice. The voice that's seeping through my bones turning them to ice. Fear crawls up my throat. I smother it with thoughts of War and his brothers just outside. This will only take a few minutes, I tell myself. Stay quiet. Wait for the Calvary as instructed. I take three deep breaths and hear him walk across the room, throwing open closet doors and turning furniture over.

"Maddie, darling, I have come to take you home."

I squeeze my eyes shut in an effort to shut out the sound of his voice.

A door slams. I think War and Orion are here. I was told to stay put until they say it's safe to open the door with the code given to me.

"Who are you?" I hear. Oh my God, it's Vi. Please run, I say silently.

"I'm here to deliver a package to Miss Maddie Holden of the Smoking Guns," Jefferson replies.

"Sorry, she's not here," Vi says, "If you want to leave it, I'll make sure she gets it."

"My orders are to deliver it directly to her," he returns.

"I can't just leave you here to wait for her," Vi volleys.

I hear footsteps. Then I hear a slap and Vi groans. "You bitch. Do you think I don't know that you and that disgusting group of sex-craved demons are the reason my pure sweet Maddie has become a whore?"

Furniture is being tossed. I know Vi is fighting to get out the door. The door slams shut. "Sit the fuck down, bitch. We'll wait for Maddie together."

I dial the emergency phone Risk installed. It's picked up immediately. "We're coming Maddie. Two minutes," I hear Orion say.

"He has Vi," I whisper. I hear him yelling at her and demanding she tell him where I am. Vi refuses and he hits her again and again. "He's hurting her. I have to help her."

"Jesus Christ what is she doing there? She is supposed to be covered," I hear the anguish in his voice. I hear her scream. Jefferson is hurting her.

"I'm going out. I can't wait. He's going to kill her."
I hang up and take the gun out of the box. I load it
like I was taught. "Never again is he going to take anything from me!"

War

I hear Orion yell in anguish. I look at him and know
that something is very wrong.

"What's wrong?" I ask.

"He's in the studio and has Vi." Orion is blaming
himself. I already see it on his face. He is reliving the
past horror only it's happening now.

We are approaching the studio. Avoiding the windows. Demon is at the back door with Risk. Cris is
climbing in through the roof to the attic. Guard is at
one window; the other brothers are spread throughout
and Orion and I are approaching the front.

The sounds of gunshots go off inside the studio.
I break down the front door to see Maddie holding
Vi in one arm and a gun in the other. Blood is splat-
tered on her clothes and hair. Vi is gripping Maddie's face. "It's okay, Honey. We're okay. You saved
us," she whispered.

The guys are all in the room. Orion is down on his
knees. Taking Vi in his arms. "Baby, what did you
do?" he says hoarsely.

I pick up Maddie and put her in my arms. She
struggles. "No, I can't leave her," she cries.

"We are bringing Vi inside the house, Kitten." I
try to console her.

She relaxes in my arms when she sees Vi in Orion's. I yell out to Cris, "Get an ambulance over here. Now."

Maddie

The nurses at the hospital are being lovely. They have been out to the waiting room several times to deliver updates. I think of the sacrifice Vi made to keep me safe. I relive that moment in my mind over and over again.

I open the panic room and aim the gun at Jefferson. "Get away from her," I scream.

"Ahh, my Maddie, my little slut," Jefferson utters. "Are you worried about your whore friend? Don't worry, I'll get rid of the demon inside of her, then I will take care of you." His slithering voice makes me want to vomit. He kicks at Vi again and again. I pull the trigger and see him stumble back. He comes at me viciously and I pull the trigger twice more. He hits the ground and I run to Vi.

"I'm so sorry, VI. I should have come out sooner. I am so sorry," I cry. I hold her close and she tells me that I saved her. She's wrong, she saved me. Vi was selfless and thought of me first. She knew I was scared and even though Jefferson was beating her, she refused to give him any information. I couldn't let her do that. I love her like a sister. I was not going to let Jefferson take her or anyone else I love from me.

War has been holding me all night. Even as we wait in the hospital, he won't let me off his lap. He keeps checking to see if I am alright. Throughout the police questioning, he stood by my side. He made me shower before heading to the hospital. I just wanted to go but he told me that it would frighten Vi to see me like that.

Orion piled into the ambulance with Vi. Guard and the brothers followed. Risk delivered all the evidence that Orion had compiled to Jefferson's plan. Demon had picked up Ava and the other old ladies and brought them to the hospital. The waiting room is filled with the Satan's Pride club members and their families.

War

When I heard the shots, I broke through the door. When I saw the blood all over her, I was terrified that Jefferson had gotten to her. I was shocked to see the hurt the Vi endured to protect Maddie. I don't know how I can ever repay her.

Orion has lost his mind. Guard was the only one to get through to him. He wouldn't let the EMT's near her, they were about to call security at the hospital when they asked him to leave the room so that they could assess the damage and get her stable. Guard was able to talk him down. Moved him into the waiting room where Ava worked her magic and stayed close to him until he was calm. Eventually, Risk was able to get him to a bathroom to wash up and get the stains of Vi's blood off his hands.

Maddie went over to him and told him how brave and loyal she was. She held his hand and leaned into his shoulder on one side as Ava did the same on the other side.

The police have all they need, and nothing will happen to Maddie. I called Paul and he is on his way home and should be back by tomorrow night. He was distraught as well but once he heard that Maddie was fine, he relaxed somewhat, still insisting on coming home.

"Anyone here for Vivianna Roslan?" A doctor walks into the room and surveys the room. Orion stands tall and takes two steps forward.

"Right here," he says roughly.

"You're her husband?" he asks.

"I'm her partner. We live together," he replies. It wasn't exactly a lie. They were together and had been for over two years. They didn't live together though.

"Want to come along with me?" the doctor asks.

"You can tell me here. These are our friends," Orion states.

"Okay," he sighs, "Vivianna has three broken ribs and a punctured lung. Fractured wrist and severe concussion. She has been stabilized and is in critical care until we see how the lung reacts. With any luck she will be moved to a regular room tomorrow. Miss Roslan has declared that she is leaving latest on Saturday. I think this is doable if she follows instructions. She is heavily sedated but has asked for Orion. I assume that is you?"

"Yeah, take me to her," Orion mutters.

"Be aware that she has tubes and is very swollen; it looks worse than it is. She may also be asleep by the time you see her," the doctor adds. "Follow me."

I know Orion, this is killing him. I hope this shit wakes him up. He has maintained his distance from any woman, even Vi. This has got to have shaken him to the core.

A few hours later, we leave the hospital. Orion is staying the night, Cris is in the waiting room to get what he needs when he needs it. Tomorrow we switch it up.

Maddie comes out of our bathroom. Sits on the edge of the bed, facing away from me. I call her to me.

"Kitten come here."

She tumbles into bed and crawls over to me. I immediately take her into me arms. "Maddie we've talked about everything that happened and you still seem distant. What's going on?"

"I'm alright."

"No, Maddie, let's get this out." I tilt her head so that we are looking into each other's eyes.

"Never again does anyone hurt me or my family," she says.

"Do not let anyone change who you are or what you do. Together we can get through anything," I say confidently.

I hold her tightly against me until I hear her breathing even out and she is sound asleep. I lay awake looking at her, knowing that she is safe in my arms.

CHAPTER 24
Celebrating New Beginnings

Maddie

The club room is beautiful. The pink plush chair for Ava is in the centre of the room with a warm blanket and pillow for back support. Of course, they are all pink with leather borders.

Vi is coming straight from the hospital and I want to ensure she is comfortable. I had a turquoise blue recliner purchased and placed next to Ava's chair. Thank the Gods for express delivery and pushy bikers. Vi's blanket and pillows are peach and raspberry colours.

Balloons in a variety of blues with silver are placed throughout the room. I have tall vases with blue and white peonies on the tables with the crystal and silverware arranged in an elegant setting. The old ladies all came over early to help me. They are wonderful. It is a great way to get to know them better and discovered how much they all love and respect Ava and Vi. The dessert table has an assortment of white and blue desserts from the bakery. They look amazing and in the centre of the table, is a two-tier baby boy biker cake. It is exceptional. The tiers have been placed off centre in an artistic manner. The mini biker jacket has the Satan's Pride insignia on the back and beneath it is written "Baby Pride". The mini motorcycle is a perfect replica of Guard's bike in tiny form. The cake is covered in black fondant with zipper half open and blue writing that says, "Welcome to Our Pride Family".

War wraps his arms around me as I'm placing the napkins on the tables. I instinctively lean back into him as I feel his tongue nip behind my ear. "Hey, Honey," I say breathlessly. It's been several days since our ordeal and we are finally settling into calm.

"Kitten, you look incredible," he whispers in my ear. I'm pretty pleased in my soft pink dress with cap sleeves and above the knee length flowy skirt. It's sweet and soft and makes me feel pretty. Even better that War thinks so too. He lets me go and turns me to him. "Vi's here, Baby. I want to remind you that though she looks really good, she still has to be careful and Orion has made it clear that she does nothing but sits and enjoys the company."

"I wouldn't dream of having her do anything," I reply with great indignation.

"I know but she will try. If she thinks of moving, Orion is going to lose his mind. So, I am asking that you all keep your eyes on her and make sure she doesn't. I'm not sure where Orion's head is at. He isn't saying much. It's almost like he has closed himself off. He is careful as hell with Vi but hasn't spoken about the day itself or how we found her," War shares.

"I promise you she won't even get the opportunity to move before what needs to be done gets done. You will have to help her to the table for lunch though," I inform him.

"Orion won't let anyone near her. He's on it," War says.

The hustle of Orion coming through the room carrying Vi pulls our attention. "Orion, I can walk," Vi announces.

"Woman, don't even think about it. You are out of the hospital against the doctor's judgement. I agreed to bring you here as long as you stay put. So, no lip," Orion says gruffly.

"Okay, big man," Vi drawls as Orion places her in her assigned blue chair. I wriggle out of War's arms and hug her gently.

"Thank you, Vi." I whisper as my eyes glisten with tears, threatening to unleash themselves. Vi pulls back and looks at me with a sly smile.

"Maddie, you saved me, remember?" she says, holding my hands.

"No Vi, I was hiding, afraid and terrified of what would happen if he found me. You challenged him and protected me. Your selflessness and strength reminded me that I have people who are willing to fight for me. It was time for me to fight for myself," I tell her.

I drape the blanket over her legs and adjust the pillows around her. "Can I get you some coffee or something?"

"I'm taking medication, that eliminates all the stuff I'd normally have," she giggles, "I'll have some coffee, though. One milk, please, if you will."

The room is filled with our guests and Vi is staying in her chair with everyone dropping by to chat with her. Orion leans against the wall, keeping his eyes on Vi. Paul and my Smoking Guns family have also joined us for the day. Paul hugs me close to him the moment he saunters into our place. He just holds me and thanks War and his brothers repeatedly for making sure I stayed safe. War invites him to stay with us in the spare room. Along with Risk, they'll overhaul the studio and bring it back to the state it was in before tragedy struck. That is next week's project; for now, Paul and the group have setup the instruments and we are going to sing the song I put together for Ava, Guard, and the baby.

Cris pops his head in the doorway. "Yo, heads up— Guard's getting her out of the truck." And as quickly as he pops in, he pops back out.

Ava steps in the room and everyone yelled "Surprise!".

Guard guides her to her princess throne where she receives hugs and kisses from everyone along the way. Ava dips down to Vi and the two women exchange a glance and hold hands as Ava settles into her chair. Her other hand reaches for me and I immediately take her hand. "This is the most perfect party I could have ever hoped for," Ava says, smiling up at me.

"Well wait for it, sister," I tell her, "We have the most amazing food for the occasion and I can't wait for you to open your gifts."

"Maddie, I have the best gifts already. I am holding the hands of the most precious gifts in my life. This is perfect. My two best friends are here and safe and healing." She smiles brightly.

"Let the party begin!" I say loudly, and everyone cheers.

The food is amazing, especially the baby sliders and the baby fries are a huge hit. Of course, we have biker-sized food for the guys, which they appreciate. The most authentic smiles erupts when Ava and Guard see the cake for the first time. Ava gushes about how beautiful it is. the first slice is cut for her and she takes a bite and give a forkful to Guard, who moans over how good it is.

"If I can have your attention," I say into the microphone. The rustling and chattering stops. "Today we are celebrating the family we have. The friendships, the loyalty, and the love we have for one another. On this special day, we celebrate a new life and new beginnings. We celebrate the impending birth of a child who will bring more joy and happiness to the Pride. I wanted to give Ava and Guard a piece of myself to thank them for all they are and all they represent to all of us. And I wanted to have this gift played over and over again so Baby Guard will hear it for years to come and know it was made just for him. I wrote this song for you guys." I walk to Guard and place the CD in his hand, then I nodded to Paul and the music begins.

I sing for them. I sing for me. As the lyrics ring out, these final words I sing for War:
What would I do without you?
Now that I see you here.

My world would be bland without you,
The colours all disappear.

I stare into my man's eyes and see that he hears me, not my voice but my soul calling to his.

It's been an amazing party. We leave the clean-up to the prospects. I argue for about a minute until I remember that this is to be expected when you join the Pride. I'm also admittedly exhausted and am looking forward to time alone with my man.

After we get home, War is waiting for me in bed. The sheet is draped over his waist and I know that he is naked underneath. I have a fluffy blue towel wrapped around me as I approach the bed.

"Drop it, Baby," War states.

I bite my lip and drop my towel.

"Over here, Kitten."

I make my way towards War. I crawl into bed and sit astride him, my legs and thighs pressed closely to his outer thighs. My breasts are level with his mouth. His hands firmly grasp my ass as his mouth closes over my nipple to suck on it. Automatically I feel a trickle of wetness between my legs. I press myself closer, but War is taking his time to lavish my breasts all the while kneading my buttocks and grinding my sex over his cock. He works me until I can barely breathe and I'm moaning and begging for him to come inside me.

"Please, Xander," I plead.

"That's right, Kitten. Here in this bed I am Xander. Always." He groans.

"My Xander, my man," I whisper against his lips.

I guide him inside me, our lips touching, moving excruciatingly slow, savouring every inch of his body.

I wrap my arms around his shoulders, feeling his thick cock growing harder, hearing the rough and ragged call of my name as I'm filled fully with my man. He holds me still. Our eyes intense with wanting, our lips connected, our bodies joined.

"I want this with you always. Every day," Xander whispers and licks my lips. He then moves my body in rhythm with his until I'm held steady and he is lifting his hips, surging deeply inside. The tension in my body is building to a fever pitch.

"Honey, I am close," I moan.

"Hold it, Baby," he utters

"I can't."

"Hold it."

"Honey, please."

I lose him as he tosses me onto my back. He enters me hard, thrusting at a relentless pace. I can't hold back any longer. My back arches off the bed, my head thrown back as I my tremble until I come. Hard. My body locks around his cock and I feel it swell and throb as Xander lets go. I open my eyes in time to see my beautiful man release himself, the sight of the corded muscle in his neck, his shoulders tense as he holds his position above me. He is perfect for me.

He kisses me passionately. Long, wet, and slow.

I could celebrate like this every day.

CHAPTER 25

The Choice is Yours

War

It's been a month, and all has settled, including me and Maddie. I have gone back to working on cars and bikes in the chop and managing the business. The brothers are breathing easier, well most of us. Orion has remained disturbed. I feel that pressure rising, and I know the lid is going to blow. We will deal with it when it happens. The brothers will be there for him as they were for Guard and me.

Maddie has spent her days working with Paul on refining the songs she wrote while he was away performing with Darren, Troy and Alex. They've all been in the studio together including Briana and Michelle. Although, I think the girls are there also hoping to hang out with Demon and Cris. Risk hasn't given them a second glance.

We spend our days doing what we love and spend the evenings and nights with each other. We have been regulars at club gatherings . Maddie has fit in so well with everyone. Her smile is contagious. Ava, Vi, and Maddie have become nearly inseparable.

Maddie's new album was released two weeks ago, and it hit the top of the charts. She has been getting requests for concerts and television appearances. She has declined them all. Paul and the rest are unhappy with her decision. Paul was pissed off enough to pay me a visit at the shop today. He laid out that he thinks that Maddie is worried about displeasing me and that I'm the reason she is holding herself back. His point may hold merit, so I heard him out and decided this is a conversation I need to have with Maddie tonight. Maddie deserves to follow her passion. I want that for her. However, I have no desire to tour the world and I have responsibilities to my shop, the people who work there, my club, and my brothers. These bonds are extremely important to me. I am not sure I want to take my life on the road when I have searched for home and family for so long.

The front door is thrown open as I park my bike. As I dismount, Maddie is rushing down the front steps and bounds towards me. I barely have time to move forward when she launches herself into my arms wraps her legs around my waist. Kisses smother my face. I walk with her in my arms as her kisses continue through the front door, which I then slam shut with a boot. I lean her back into the door and take her mouth ferociously, pressing into her body so she can feel me.

I lift her skirt, slipping my hands beneath it to cup her ass with one hand all the while ripping at her panties until they are torn from her and I have all access to her sweet pussy. I circle her clit, causing a whimper to escape her lips that are fused to mine. My cock aches against the zipper of my jeans. I slide my hand between us freeing myself from my confined clothing and resume showering my woman with long passionate kisses, my fingers teasing and torturing her body.

Then she says the words I love to hear when she is so consumed with need, "Give me you, Xander. Please, I need you now," she begs.

"How do you want it, Baby?" I delay her a little longer as I nip at the spot on her neck that drives her over the edge.

"Hard and fast, Honey. And now," she says with desperation as she sinks her fingers into my hair, gripping it hard.

I thrust into her in one fluid motion. A gasp pours from her perfect mouth, then she squirms to accommodate my length. I continue to pound her pussy and can feel her muscles contract and her breast heave.

"Eyes on me, Kitten. I want to see you come," I moan through clenched teeth. I am on the verge and holding on by a thread.

She explodes in my arms and with one final thrust, I come inside her. I hold her steady until we both catch our breath. I pull out gently and walk her over to the armchair with Maddie still sitting astride my lap. I put myself back together and slide her skirt down over her ass.

Her bright smile fills my sight. "Did you have a good day?" she giggles.

I burst out in laughter. "Great day. Even better now."

No time like the present to attack the situation I've had on my mind since Paul walked into the garage this afternoon. "Maddie, I want to talk to you. Your brother came to see me today. He is upset that you haven't changed your mind about doing concerts and appearances."

"Xander.," she interrupts.

"No wait. Hear me out. If you have decided that you like things as they are, and this is as much as you want to give to your music, then I will stop right now. Before you say anything, I want to point out that you love singing. You love the music, the audience; you are a naturally talented performer. You have nothing to fear. I will get you the best security around." I glide my hand across her brow and tuck a stray ringlet behind her ear. "However, I will not be able to join you on a tour. I have responsibilities here and I have a life that I have built with roots and family. At best, I would be able to meet you in certain places once a month. I won't like us being apart; I will truly hate it, but I want you to have it all. I don't want you to miss out because you feel torn between."

"Stop." Maddie places her fingers over my lips. "Let me tell you what I want." Her arms circle my neck and she dips in close to me. "I want to wake up every morning with you and fall asleep beside you every night. Yes, I love to sing, however, not having you there with me gives me no one to sing to. Now if you tell me that you can manage one weekend a month, then I will commit to twelve appearances. I don't need or want more. The more I am away, the less time I have to write." Her lips brush mine softly.

"The choice is yours, Maddie. I want you to have it all," I tell her. My throat is filled with emotion and I manage to croak out the words.

"I already have it all, right here with you."

"If this ever changes, you tell me, and we will figure it out."

"Not going to happen but thank you for leaving the door open," she murmurs.

"Alright, Baby. I love you," I tell her.

Her cheeky smile lights up, "I know. I love you too." She straightens. "We have to get ready, Honey. Right before you got here, Guard called, Ava is at the hospital having her baby. We have to go meet them there."

"I'll take a quick shower in the spare bathroom. You get washed up too and we'll head out in fifteen minutes." I know that if we shower together there is no way we will make it out of here anytime soon.

CHAPTER 26

Birth of Change

Maddie

We are back at the same hospital as we were a month ago, except this time it's for a joyous occasion. All the brothers are sitting, leaning, or pacing in the waiting room. Vi and I are sitting side by side. Vi has recovered well. She is finishing up the last of her physiotherapy and is back at work at Millie's place. We have grown very close.

Guard marches through the doors, beaming from ear to ear. We stand and approach him, War guiding me to the front along with Vi.

"It's a healthy boy," he confirms. "He's perfect."

"Ava?" Vi asked.

"She's doing great. She was amazing," Guard says.

"What's his name?" War asks.

"Gavin," he replied and looks directly at Orion, who locked eyes with Guard. A silent conversation is taking place. The rest of crew looks between them. It's true. They all speak a secret language that only they understand.

Vi walks over to Orion and wraps her arms around his waist. Looking up at his tall form, she pulls him down so that she can kiss his cheek.

"Only two people can go in to see her at a time and she has asked for Orion ad Vi, then War and Maddie. She wants to see you all though, so be patient," Guard says.

War pulls me over to a chair and guides me onto his lap while we wait our turn.

Orion and Vi come back through. I hear him say, "I'll have Demon drop you at home. I have something to do tonight. Call you tomorrow." He walks out, and Vi's eyes followed him through the exit. She drops her head. I wanted to go and talk to her, but War is tugging on my hand towards Ava's room.

"Stay out of it, Kitten. This is between them." He reads my mind.

I sigh in frustration. I know he's right. It's so hard to see Vi this way.

"Baby, let's go enjoy the moment with Guard, Ava, and Gavin."

The baby is magnificent. He has Guard's eyes and Ava's lips with dark fuzzy hair. He is perfect. I hold him in my arms, cooing and whispering to him. I begin to sing his song; his eyes blink themselves closed and he drifts to sleep in my arms.

War teases Guard, "Your life is forever going to change."

"Change is constant, War. Birth is change and I happily accept it," Guard declares.

I look over at Ava. "Today, life is perfect," she said.

War holds me close and I look up at him. Words aren't necessary; we both know that together, we can overcome anything. Change is imminent. We feel it coming, we will brace for it and work together. Nothing comes between us from this point on.

About The Author

A.G. KIRKHAM knows romance! Born in one of the most romantic countries in the world, Italy! Her family migrated to Canada when she was a young girl, and she quickly fell in love with reading and writing. Her favorite time in school was getting lost in the books. That feeling has never left. And she has been writing short stories and poems from an early age.

Her world is filled with off-beat friends and family who make her life zany and unique—all the better for enhancing the creativity in her work! She was always the "good" girl growing up, but somewhere along the way her "rebel' girl has emerged in her books and in life. She is the author of the popular Satan's Pride series including Guard, and now War, where each book represents the belief that love truly exists!

Follow her book series at www.romancebyagkirkham.com

www.ingramcontent.com/pod-product-compliance
Lightning Source LLC
Chambersburg PA
CBHW061236210726
48293CB00003B/790